THE DARK LEGION

WE THE MUTANTS
BOOK 2

Stella Fitzsimons

Books by Stella Fitzsimons

Mist Riders

Luna
Winter
Silver Dust
Shadow Fall
Moonlight Mist
The Last Rider

We the Mutants

Forest Runners
The Dark Legion
The Shadow Empire
Beyond the River of Time
Rise of the Saviors
We the Mutants Origins

THE DARK LEGION

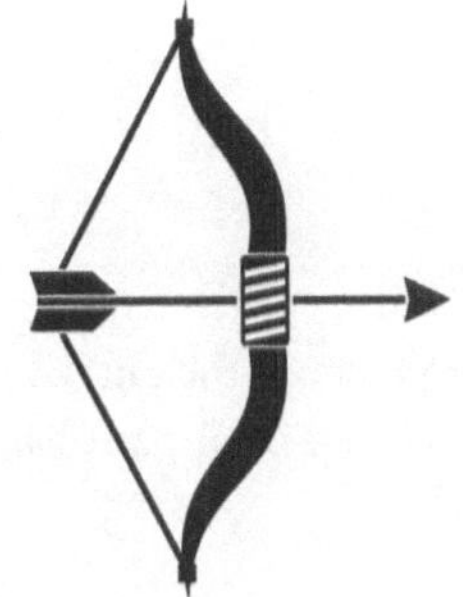

We the Mutants

For Daniel...

CHAPTER 1

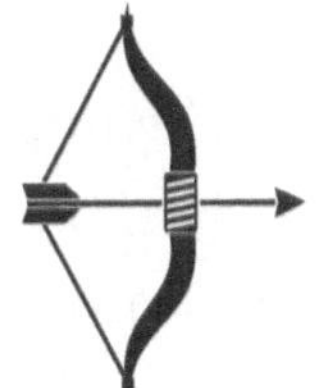

I CAN FEEL PIP's heartbeat pounding in her small ribcage. I hold her close. We must keep still. The cranberry bushes have only just blossomed. A stroke of luck. Their thick branches will conceal us.

Pip pinches my hand and points toward the fir trees a few feet away.

"Not yet," I whisper. "We'll be safe here if we keep quiet." When I kiss the top of her head, she pinches me harder than before.

I follow her gaze to see what she sees—a long shadow crawling slowly across the top of the honeysuckle near the fir trees. We must not move or speak. I press my hand over Pip's mouth. We sink lower into the bushes. I search for tiny openings to see through the leaves, trying to locate the beast that hunts us.

We hear a loud thud behind us. Pip's eyes panic. Something has landed close by and is moving toward us. The crackling of dry twigs grows louder, getting closer and closer. Pip breaks free and before I can stop her, she stands.

Ice explodes in my veins. "Run," I yell. "Run!"

We dart out of the bushes, blindly heaving ourselves forward, trying not to run into the trees as we flee. Pip is small but fast. She holds her own in our race to safety. We pick up cuts and scratches as we dash madly, hoping to make it to the training ring. There's a hut there where the Saviors keep weapons. A dozen more strides and we'll make it.

The long shadow catches us, covering up the small part of sky that is visible through the branches. The world gets darker. The beast must be reaching for us now. Our fragile bodies brace for its sharp fingers when, suddenly, the creature lands hard on the ground ahead of us, cutting off our path to the hut.

The huge black figure looms over us for a split second, then charges. Pip lets out a cry. I rush forward to hurl myself between her and the assailant.

"That's enough," I shout, but it's too late. The massive body collides into us. We fall to the ground in a heap of twisted arms and legs.

"Shy Boy," I yell, "you'll squeeze us to death!"

Shy Boy retreats and taps the top of his head to show

that he's sorry, but a moment later he falls to the ground, rubbing his tummy and laughing.

Pip follows suit soon afterward and I laugh at them both. The tiny twelve-year-old girl and the gigantic, ferocious-looking black chimpanzee.

Pip and I met Shy Boy during one of our walks in the woods weeks ago. We spotted him from a distance while he was trying to relieve the itch on his back by rubbing it against a trunk. Pip didn't know what to make of this until I explained to her that there were chimpanzees roaming free in the forests.

Pip moved closer to take a good look at Shy Boy. When he saw her, he ran and hid behind the tree. Pip got even closer and extended her arm to him.

I followed her, getting as close to Shy Boy as possible. "Hey you," I said. "It's okay, you don't have to be scared. We're nice. We come in peace and friendship."

Shy Boy stuck his neck out and stared at us. Then he quickly pulled his head back behind the tree.

"I see, you're just a shy boy," I said.

I reached inside my pocket and took out a handful of walnuts. That made Shy Boy increasingly restless until in the end, he had no option but to come out of his hiding. He took the walnuts off the palm of my hand slowly and with great respect. Pip and I walked away to give him some privacy.

The next time we came upon him, Shy Boy only took

a few seconds to accept an apple from Pip. By the third time, he practically jumped on us. He has been our shadow ever since. He seems to like his name. He responds right away when we call him. His friendship makes Pip happy and I'm all for that.

In the two months since we found her, Pip has barely uttered a word. Doc says there's nothing wrong with her mentally or physically. She will say simple things happily, mostly terms of politeness like *please* and *thank you*, but never a full sentence. She will not answer questions or ask them. She's cheerful, sweet and polite but little else. All other things are too much for her.

The horrors of the world are lost to Pip. She wants no part of them. Who can blame her? *We have to be patient*, Doc says. She is blocked somehow. We can only hope for the best.

Shy Boy sniffs around our pockets, smelling the pumpkin seeds that are hidden there. We empty the contents, and he gulps them down.

"Wow, you're fast," I say. "You're so hungry, aren't you?" I talk to him as if he were a baby, as if he needed to be protected. He rubs his nose against my arm and kisses it.

Finn comes to us with a grin on his face. "I knew I'd find you here." He hands a piece of bread to Shy Boy. "You can't feed this guy fast enough," he says as Shy Boy licks his fingers.

I immediately come to Shy Boy's defense. "He's huge, he needs a lot of food."

"Yeah. Just don't let Damian know how much. He'll go—"

"Red!" I finish the sentence for Finn. "He won't know and if he does, so be it. How can anyone look into Shy Boy's eyes and not fall in love with him?"

"In love with a chimpanzee. Yep, it sounds like you," Finn teases.

"Careful, you sound jealous."

He pays no attention to me. He turns to Pip. "Hey, Pip, do you think you might try and talk a little today?"

She shakes her head.

"Whenever you're ready," Finn says. "We're not going anywhere."

Despite her small size, Pip is very strong and can withstand any hardship. At twelve, she is incredibly smart. Even Zoe has a hard time competing with her when it comes to math equations and problem solving.

Shy Boy drops heavily to the ground and Pip climbs onto his lap. I lie down next to them and let my head rest on a bed of pine needles. Finn lies beside me. He points at a small patch of blue within the branches above.

"Someday, Tick," he says, "we will be able to fly."

"You mean like birds?"

"No! I mean on planes and airships."

"Ah. You think Theo will find a way to make it happen."

"Of course. It's his life's passion right now. Find plane, repair plane, fly plane."

A small plane or a helicopter would make all the difference in the world. The invaders don't use flying vehicles on our planet. The occasional aircrafts gliding across the sky seem to be transport ships, silent and rare like comets. Give us a few operational, armed airships and the balance of forces would definitely shift. We could fight back. We could have them looking up, make them fear us for a change.

"Dreams are good," I say.

Finn takes my hand. "Yes, it's good to be able to dream," he says and then suddenly tickles me.

"Finn, stop it! You know I can't take tickling. My reflexes will take charge and I'll hurt you," I say, laughing miserably.

Shy Boy starts tickling Pip. She jumps out of his lap and gets between Finn and me. Finn attacks her immediately, knocking all three of us back onto the ground.

"Alright, that's enough," Rabbit's voice cuts in, but Pip quickly grabs his leg and, before he knows it, Rabbit finds himself on the ground with us.

"Guys, seriously, you have to get back. Doc is looking for you, Freya. You said to get you right away if he asked for you."

Shy Boy leaps away at this and Pip laughs. Shy Boy is afraid of Doc's name ever since Doc tried to take a blood sample from him.

We walk back to our camp which is nestled within a green oasis on the side of the mountain we currently call home. This won't be forever, but we will enjoy it while it lasts. The temperatures are cooler here and the crystal-clear spring water is delicious.

The camp is small compared to our previous dwellings. There are seven large tents and all of them are shared except that of Damian and that of Doc who needs a lot of room for his medical experiments and also to see his patients. I share mine with Pip. Finn stays with Rabbit. Tilly and Scout share the third one. Zoe stays with Nya, which leaves Biscuit with Theo.

We've placed our tents in a semi-circle in front of the big cave that we use for almost everything: meetings, cooking, eating and hanging out. There's also an area to store Theo's devices—what he has left of them anyway. The only power source he has available is the one I can produce with my sensory receptor device and I'm not doing a very consistent job with it.

Nya hangs outside the cave with Tilly. They both nod at us.

"Doc's inside," Tilly says, trying to hide her excitement.

Nya stares at Pip for a moment before she pats me on the shoulder.

We step inside the cave. All twelve are here. With Pip we are still twelve, but Daphne's absence is always felt.

Damian comes to me, deeply concerned. "The energy levels are very low today, we can barely get the cooling system to run," he says. "Will you be able to use the receptor later?"

I nod but I realize that's not what concerns him. I walk over to where Doc sits. "You wanted to see me?"

"I do, yes," Doc says as his eyes get bigger and brighter. "I was able to perform a partial DNA profiling with the kits that Rabbit found in Lost Town which I think provides sufficient information, albeit incomplete."

My heart soars and my knees feel weak at Doc's words. "And?"

"You were right," Doc says. "Pip is your biological sister. There's no question about it; you share a number of markers that are unique."

I have known that since the very first time I set my eyes on Pip. She looks so much like our mother but there's also something else about her, something that I can't quite put my finger on, that is extremely familiar.

Damian insisted that we needed concrete proof and he has been suspicious since day one. His suspicions became all the more worrisome when Pip punched the words *"they let me go"* on my touchpad after he asked her how she had managed to escape.

We have been through this a million times. He keeps telling me not to get invested in Pip until we know what's going on, but now that there's proof she's my sister, maybe he will lighten up a bit.

Pip hugs me and I feel her love expanding inside her little body. Nothing could tear us apart. I look at Finn and he gives me a smile. There are three of us here from our village now. Finn will protect Pip with his life, the way he has always done for me.

"We should celebrate this," Tilly suggests.

"Yes, maybe we can bake cookies and a pie," Biscuit says.

Tilly slaps him gently on the back. "Didn't we do that yesterday? There's plenty left."

"You can never have enough cookies or pie," Biscuit insists.

"Oh, come on, Biscuit," Rabbit says. "You don't have to use the same joke all the time."

Biscuit becomes perplexed. "I never joke about food."

Zoe comes to me. "Are you happy?" she says. I can see she is touched by what has been revealed today.

"I am, Zoe. For the first time in my life, I can honestly say that."

Zoe understands how I feel because of Theo whom she loves like a younger brother. Besides Finn and me, they are the only ones that share the same background, having both been harvested for Plantation-1.

"I wish Daphne was here," Zoe says. "She would have liked that. She told me many times she wished she'd have a little sister."

Zoe's voice breaks. She misses Daphne a lot. We all do, but with Zoe the loss is more urgent and present. We have become closer the past few weeks, Zoe and I, and she has proven to be a very wise and honest friend.

"We will carry her with us and make sure she didn't die in vain," I say even though I know it's not much of a consolation.

❖

"Pip was sent to us for a reason," Damian says when we sit down for supper in the evening. "Whatever that reason was, it's up to us to turn it into something positive, something that will bring stability to our group." He turns to Pip. "You are an official member of the Saviors, Pip. You may never be safe, but you will never be alone."

CHAPTER 2

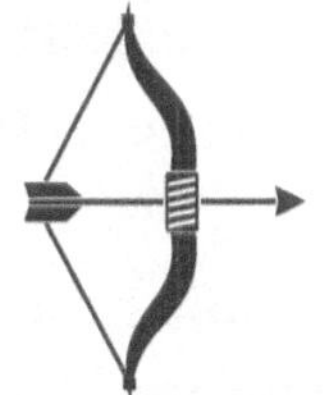

ANY NOTION OF AN interrogation would have normally been enough to set me off running for shelter and covering up my tracks. As it is, I've had to agree with Damian that it is of crucial importance to have Pip try to remember as much as she can from Plantation-15. Damian doesn't leave anything to chance. I have come to appreciate this quality about him.

We are gathered in Damian's tent—Pip, Finn, Doc and I. Pip doesn't remember much. She has big holes in her memory, and I don't like to watch her struggle to remember to no avail. They did something to her. Any mention of the Sliman or the plantation brings distress to her eyes. Unfortunately, our only hope of discovering what happened to her is to help Pip remember.

Pip's brown hair has grown a lot since we found her. The two distinct colors in her eyes that startled me at first (black and azure) have blended into a beautiful dark blue. She is graceful in her movements and although she hasn't demonstrated any special abilities, she has shown considerable skill at many things. She is quick, agile and intuitive. She can learn new skills with a fair amount of ease. She doesn't like pulse guns, but she is very accurate with a shock bow.

"Let's go over it one more time," Damian says. "How exactly did you leave the plantation?"

Pip types out what we already know. A guard took her away from a group of children while they were practicing. He escorted her to the back of the library building. There, two more Sliman were waiting. All three got Pip out of the plantation through a back gate. They had a vehicle waiting. They dropped Pip in the field where we found her. When Pip hesitated and tried to get back on the vehicle, they pushed her out and drove away. It wasn't until after we located her that she realized it caused a horrible feeling inside when she tried to speak. Something worse than fear. Simple words she can manage. Anything else at all terrifies her and she starts to shake.

"Is it because of the shock, Pip?" Damian asks her. "Did something happen to you? Did you say something you shouldn't have maybe?"

Pip shrugs and types that she can't be sure. She can't remember what happened with the Sliman on the way to the field. And she can only recall glimpses of what the insides of the buildings in the plantation looked like. Parts of her memory have been blocked or erased.

"It's as if they didn't want her to give away anything about Plantation-15," Damian says. "But they did want us to find her. They have a plan."

Finn nods. "Do you think we should keep moving?"

"I honestly don't know," Damian says. "Doc, is it possible that there's a tracking chip in her?"

"There's no way for me to tell," Doc says. "Not without a full body scan."

Tracking chips can be so small they are almost invisible. They can be implanted through the mouth and ears, or with an injection straight inside the bone marrow. We don't have the equipment that could locate a thing like that.

"Don't talk about Pip as if she's not here," I say.

"Pip understands the importance of the situation, Tick," Finn says. "She wants answers, too. Give her some credit."

Damian puts his hand on Finn's shoulder. His eyes betray puzzlement.

"What is it?" Finn says, staring at Damian's hand.

"What did you just call her?"

"Who?"

"What do you mean, *who*? Freya, or should I say *Tick*? What the hell is Tick?"

"Don't tell him, Finn," I say, exasperated.

Tick. Short for ticklish, Pip types. *Freya told me. On the plantation. It was Finn's name for her.*

Damian removes his hand from Finn's shoulder. "Thank you, Pip," he says while looking at me. "Finally, someone in the family who can give a straight answer."

It's nice to see some things never change. He can still drive me crazy with his arrogance.

❖

MY HAND FEELS TIGHT and tense around the sensory receptor. I always get a bit nervous before I have to use it. I can feel how the energy enters my body like a mild electroshock before it takes me over completely. I wonder if this is similar to what happens to Pip when she tries to speak. The device gets attached to my nerve endings and then multiple signals start traveling up and down the channel that has been established. My mind sends orders to the receptor and the receptor sends reports to my brain.

I have not been able to completely control the relationship yet. In fact, the more I use the receptor, the more it seems like it's the one in control, not me.

Theo has been working with me to help me learn how to channel the energy the way I want. I'm hoping that the day will come soon when I will learn to be in absolute command of its capabilities.

Maybe Pip can learn to control what's happening inside of her, too.

I embrace myself for what is about to come once I order the receptor to switch on and produce the blue energy that Theo will be able to convert into electricity. I stand next to the generator in the small clearing to the west of the camp. I close my eyes and concentrate.

The energy enters my bloodstream, and a series of white flashing lights blur my vision. The generator starts humming and I know the connection has been established. I need to keep doing this for a few minutes before the camp is powered up again.

"It's good to see you haven't lost your superhero powers yet," I hear Damian's voice behind me. It startles me. My heartbeat gets faster and I get an instant headache as the receptor suddenly turns off.

"Damn it, Damian, what are you doing? Are you trying to kill me?"

"Believe me, if I wanted you dead—"

"Yeah, yeah, I'd be dead by now. You have all the charm of a Sliman." I rub my arms vigorously to get my blood going again. Everything feels numb.

He hands me his flask of warm green tea. I take a sip and glance at him, trying to guess what he's doing here.

"So, he has a special name for you," he says.

I knew he was not going to pass on a chance to make fun of me. "Is that a problem?"

"No, not a problem at all."

"So drop it already."

I hand him back the flask of tea and shake the receptor as if trying to determine whether it will work again or not.

I steal a glance at Damian. "What are you waiting for? Go. I can't concentrate with you staring at me."

"You're ticklish," he says as a wide grin forms on his lips. "On top of everything."

"You're getting weird again."

"For someone as secretive as you, you've allowed Finn to know a whole lot about you."

I fear where this is going. "I've known Finn all my life. Of course we know things about each other."

"Just how ticklish are you exactly?"

It hits me that he's here to tickle me. Or at least try. I see the amused expression on his face. I don't like it because it's not consistent with who he is, but also because I want to avoid thinking about the night that he kissed me at all costs. It brings up too many painful memories, too many regrets. I need normalcy in my life more than anything else right now.

"Oh no, you don't," I say as he drops the flask and moves in to put his plan to work. I try to run away, but he catches up with me quite easily.

"I'm holding the receptor and I will use it if I have to," I warn him, but he doesn't take my threat seriously. There are a few dead Sliman who made the same mistake.

His fingers attack my midsection. The shock of being tickled sends me crashing off balance immediately. I drop to my knees and twist away from his reach.

He follows me down, and I can tell that his fingers aim at my neck. Before I can think about it, I turn the receptor on him and blast him away with a surge of violet energy that lifts him a few feet off the ground. I turn off the receptor and Damian crashes back to earth with a thud.

I rush to his side, mortified. "Damian, did I hurt you?"

He groans a little, but before I can check if he's hurt, he comes at me with full force. His left hand clamps around both my wrists while his right zeroes in on my most ticklish spots. I fall back, writhing with uncontrollable laughter. He climbs on top of me, pinning me down, his merciless fingers never pausing their attack for even a second. I think I'm having a déjà vu from yesterday when Finn attacked me in the same way.

"I can't breathe," I protest, but he is relentless. I could kill them both, I think, and that would be the end of the tickling.

"Damian?" It's Tilly's voice. Yep, it's déjà vu alright.

Damian stops to look at her. Tilly and Biscuit watch us in bewilderment. What an odd image we must make—sweaty and rolling on the ground with our faces flustered.

"What's going on?" Damian says as he sits up.

I do my best to straighten my hair and my shirt, cursing under my breath for having allowed Damian to get his way with me once again.

"Ah, three Sliman are here and they're asking for you," Biscuit says.

"Seriously, Biscuit, what's going on?" Damian scolds him.

"He just told you," Tilly says. "We were practicing outside the cave when the Sliman appeared out of nowhere. We reached for our guns, but they dropped theirs, raised their arms and said that they've come in peace. Then they asked to talk to our leader."

Damian's face grows pale. "It's begun," he says as he draws his gun. "Freya, keep your receptor out of sight, but keep your fingers on it."

We rush to the camp. The receptor burns in my pocket and my fingers feel heavy and slick with sweat as they curl around it.

The scene unfolds exactly as Tilly and Biscuit described it, yet it's somehow even more unsettling in person. Three huge Sliman warriors stand in the middle of the camp clad in long black cloaks that cover their powerful frames from head to toe. Their bright green eyes shine in a ghostly manner beneath their hoods, tracking every movement with predatory focus. The skin on their hands is marked with tattoos in geometric patterns.

Their pulse guns and curved shock bows lie on the

ground behind Finn, who keeps his own pulse gun trained on them.

One of the Sliman steps forward. He's taller than the others and moves with an air of undeniable command—the leader of the group no doubt.

His gaze lands on Damian. "There you are," he says. His voice, deep and resonant, sounds jarringly normal. There's nothing alien about it, no strange intonation, no eerie echo, no distorted growling. It could be the voice of any big, strong man. "You must be the leader."

And you are?" Damian asks.

"Wudak," the Sliman replies with a slight incline of his head. "We come to you in peace."

Damian shakes his head. "And why the hell should I trust a Sliman?"

"Hear us out. Then you can make that decision."

"Speak then."

Wudak tilts his head. "Shouldn't we do this in private?"

"No," Damian says. "We're all equal here, but, of course, this is something you would never understand."

A sly smile forms on Wudak's lips. "No, you are not all equal." His gaze slides past Damian to fix directly on me. "We have come to pledge our loyalty to you," he says. "You will be our queen. And we will serve you as you wish."

Stunned, I stumble backward as all three Sliman warriors advance toward me with bowed heads.

Damian jumps to action, slamming the butt of his pulse

gun into Wudak's face, then banging the heads of the other two Sliman together before they can react.

"Get the hell away from her," he snarls.

Wudak straightens slowly, wiping blood from his face with unsettling calm. "So the word is true," he says. "You have the strength of a Sliman."

Damian pays no attention to him. "Finn," he says, "tie them up."

CHAPTER 3

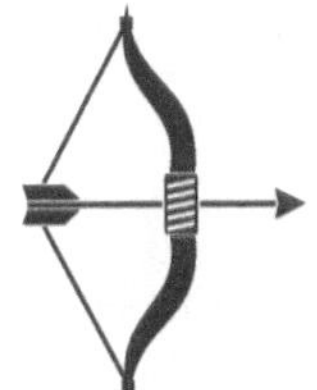

THE SLIMAN WARRIORS' HANDS are tied behind their backs with polymer cords. Damian drives them forward with a pulse gun in each hand, forcing them into the part of the cave that serves as our command center. Nya stands guard at the entrance. Her tall frame is drawn taut like a fine bowstring, her muscles are primed for action and all her senses are sharpened.

Damian forces the three Sliman to sit on the stone floor in front of Theo's heavy desk. He binds their legs together before tying them to each other. The Sliman don't resist this; they don't even blink when Damian yanks back their hoods with unnecessary force.

The one named Wudak has long black hair that falls past his shoulders with two thin braids framing his face. There's an unnatural elegance to him that makes my skin crawl. He's handsome in a way that feels *too* precise, too deliberate—sharp, symmetrical features with angular cheekbones and a strong jawline. His expression shifts with calculated smoothness, as though each micro-movement has been programmed rather than felt.

The other two have shorter brown hair, and their features are just as sharp and unreadable, as if they were all cast from the same mold.

All three bear identification patterns tattooed in gray ink around the corners of their glowing green eyes. The detailed calligraphy of the markings signifies high rank among their kind, and Wudak's in particular are the most elaborate, curling in delicate strokes that extend to his temples.

They all appear the same age, perhaps thirty to thirty-five by human standards, but then again so do all Sliman. They never seem to age, they never change. The prevailing theory is that when they do—*if* they do—they're simply decommissioned, discarded like the humans in the breeding villages.

"How did you find us?" Damian says as he draws a serrated combat knife from his boot.

"You don't need to be aggressive," Wudak says. "We are here to explain things to you. So that you understand."

"How. Did. You. Find. Us?" Damian repeats, pausing between words for effect.

"I am Wudak," the Sliman says. "Commander of the third Sliman Regiment on Plantation-15." He tilts his head slightly toward his companions. "This is Malzod, and this is Gritu."

Gritu is the smallest of the three but still massive compared to us. Only Damian comes close to matching his imposing physicality.

Damian is about to strike Wudak again when I lunge forward and grasp his wrist. The corded muscles there are tense under my fingers. "Let him talk," I plead with him.

Damian's eyes find mine, confusion battling with anger in their depths. For a moment, I think he'll shake me off.

"She's right, Damian. Let's hear what they have to say," Finn says.

Damian lowers his hand. "Talk," he growls at Wudak.

Wudak turns his face toward Pip. "We have been following you," he says.

I search for Finn's eyes. It all makes sense now, but knowing the truth isn't much of a comfort. Quite the opposite.

"You released the little girl." Damian is the one to say it out loud. The truthness of his words bounces off the walls of the cave like a distant echo. "You've placed some tracking chip on her. That's how you knew where to find us. That's why you let her go. To set a trap for us."

Wudak shakes his head. "We freed her as a gesture of our goodwill. So you would know we are truthful." He says those last words looking at me. His eyes make me feel more than a little uncomfortable.

"You knew she was my sister," I whisper.

"Yes. And we destroyed all evidence that could connect her to you."

I consider this for a moment. "I have two sisters," I say.

"No, you don't. Not anymore. Otherwise, she would be here as well. You have my word for it."

I cover my mouth with my hand. Pip's eyes well up and her fingers pull on my shirt. Finn tries to put his arms around me, but I push him away. I've known that my brother must have either vanished or been lobotomized by now, but my sister was young enough to be in a plantation still.

"How?" I say. "How did she die?"

"I see that I have upset you. I am sorry. I keep forgetting how sensitive humans are," Wudak says before he lowers his head.

"Is this the kind of crap we have to listen to?" Damian snaps. It's clear he would want nothing more than to kill them right now. Maybe in his mind that would be a way to avenge Daphne's death.

"There has to be some point to all this," Finn says. He turns to Wudak. "Is there a point? I don't like your chances if you don't get to it fast."

"We are here to protect the queen with the sensory receptor," Wudak says. "She is in danger."

"My name is Freya," I say, trying to hold back my tears.

Wudak nods. "Freya, you are in grave danger. We have

come to protect you and offer our allegiance."

I can feel how my companions shift their positions, how they stare at the Sliman in shock, disbelief and fear. Tilly's hand finds mine. Her fingers feel ice-cold against my skin.

Damian grabs a fistful of Wudak's hair and pulls it back as if trying to rip it off until the Sliman's throat is exposed. "What kind of danger? And why would you care?"

"Because we are slaves just like humans. And because we don't like it," Wudak says, staring into Damian's eyes.

"Bullshit," Damian spits out.

Wudak turns his gaze back to me. "The Lagerian masters, they don't want you to know what you are capable of doing, but we know. We can show you. We can teach you. We can help you win."

My heart hammers. There's only one thing that matters right now. "Is my sister dead?"

"We don't have that information," Wudak says. "What we know is that she is out of the plantation network, and that is never a good thing."

"What happens when kids leave the plantations? Where do they go?" Damian asks. It's the question we have all been asking since the day we were able to talk.

"I will tell you what I know when the time comes. You have to trust us first. It is true that I don't know everything though."

"This all sounds a little too convenient," Damian says. His forehead tenses as he arches his eyebrows.

"There's nothing convenient about what we're doing. If the Lagerians suspect there's an insurgency building up within the Sliman ranks, they will destroy us on the spot."

Finn shakes his head. "You're stronger than them, you know how they operate, what their weaknesses are. This whole time we've thought you were brainless, but it's obvious now that there's a high degree of intelligence in you. Why not use what you know to bring the aliens down and free yourselves? Why come to us? Why are you seeking out Freya?"

Wudak sighs and his companions lower their heads as if responding to an unspoken command. "We are not as lucky as you," he says. "We do not enjoy the gift of autonomy. We depend on the aliens for our survival."

Doc is intrigued by that. "What do you mean?"

"Once a month we receive an injection. It's called Omicron 5, and we believe it's composed of different minerals, perhaps from different planets, and some forms of highly specialized bacteria. That combination keeps us alive. Without it, all our body systems start to shut down one after the other. Organ failure. Neural collapse. Death. Only the aliens know how to prepare the formula, and only the sensory receptors can bind it into a transmittable fluid."

Malzod shifts uncomfortably, the first independent movement I've seen from him.

"The aliens produce the minimum amount that is

needed for one month, so that we can never accumulate additional supplies," Wudak continues. "We could attempt to steal a sample and have it analyzed, but even if we managed to analyze and recreate it, which is doubtful, it would be useless without the receptor."

"Without someone who can yield the power inside it," Finn concludes, glancing at me.

"So this is all about you. You need Freya for her powers. The rest is a smokescreen," Damian says. His voice drips with disgust.

Gritu speaks for the first time. "What we are trying to say is that we have a common enemy. We are earthlings now, just like you. We were born on this planet, just like you. We want to be free, just like you. There is room for everyone."

"We need you and you need us," Wudak says. "You'll never beat the aliens without our help. Trust us on this. A thousand receptors would not be enough."

Silence overtakes the cave as we try to determine whether what the Sliman warriors say can be trusted or not. Even Tilly is stunned into muteness.

"Why did you say that Freya is in danger? What was that all about?" Damian wants to know.

"There's nothing that the aliens want more than to get their hands on her right now." Wudak's words sink in slowly, turning my blood to ice. "They have been preparing for you, Freya. They will come for you. And they will try to take you by surprise."

"Do they know where we are?" Damian says.

"No, but that will change soon."

"Why? Are you going to tell them?"

"I understand that you want to protect your companions, that you want to protect Freya, but if you don't listen to me, you will all be captives again. Or dead. Soon."

Damian begins to lose the little patience he has left. "You're in no position to make threats."

"The Lagerians are bringing in their drone air vehicles," Wudak says. "There's no escaping those things. They will scan the entire district within hours, or even minutes if they get lucky. They will pick up your position and they will blow you up, but not before they have captured Freya."

"Where are those aircrafts?" Theo says. "We have never seen them."

"They are on their way to Earth as we speak. They are being transferred by two massive cargospheres. The drones run on synthetic fuel that cannot be found or composed here. They have to bring in the fuel, too. Normally, they wouldn't do that because certain elements in the Earth's atmosphere can cause the fuel to explode. But they will risk it on this one occasion. That's how much they want you eliminated."

I turn to Finn. I can see that he, too, remembers our conversation from yesterday. There's no time to dream about planes anymore. Not if what we're hearing is true.

Theo's face has sunk. Zoe puts one consoling arm around him. Tilly holds Biscuit's hand.

Something is going on between those two, I think, as if trying to disentangle myself from the horrible news by sticking to simple thoughts.

"I still don't know why we should believe any of this," Damian says.

"We have already said a lot more than we should have. We have taken a great risk by coming here. By letting you know about the Omicron 5," Wudak says.

Damian shakes his head. "It's not enough."

Wudak thinks for a moment. His eyes narrow down to slits as he's evaluating the situation. Then he takes a long glance at each of his companions. Both Malzod and Gritu nod reluctantly as if giving him permission for something.

"As you wish," Wudak says. "If I am honest, I've always known it would come to this. You want proof that we are sincere. How would you like to kill a few aliens?"

His words produce the desired effect. We can barely breathe. Scout and Rabbit both exclaim in unison, "We'd like that!"

Damian can't shake his doubts. "What do you mean *kill a few aliens*?"

"We can help you attack a Lagerian convoy that will pass through the district's lowland tomorrow. We can tell you all you need to know to turn the encounter into a complete and absolute victory."

Damian is clearly intrigued by the possibility. He raises his eyebrows the way he always does when he sniffs out opportunity.

Finn gets fidgety—he shifts his weight from leg to leg, trying to calm himself down. I know he has a million things he wants to ask Wudak. I take his hand in mine to steady him. Even Nya drops her post and comes closer.

"I'm listening," Damian says.

"Three aliens are leaving Plantation-9 and Earth," Wudak begins but is interrupted by Biscuit.

"Terrible place," he says as he reminisces Plantation-9. "Horrible food."

Wudak doesn't know what to make of this. He continues after a short pause. "They will travel to a predetermined landing area a few miles north of the plantation. They will carry equipment and food to take back with them. There are several spots along the way where you could attack them."

"What about a Sliman escort?" Finn asks.

"Yes, there will be one. Eight guards. You can take them if you surprise them. And you will. They won't see you coming."

"You'd have us kill your own kind?" Damian says, disgusted.

"They're not our kind. They're killing machines," Wudak says, staring into Damian's puzzled eyes.

"If only you knew how much bloodshed there has been among humans," Gritu says. "Genocides, holocausts, civil wars. There's always some reason behind it—most of them illogical. How do you think the aliens were able to take over this planet? Humans were not unified. They were already weakened by a war over a primitive energy source called oil. They were killing each other before the first alien ship arrived."

Wudak shoots Gritu a warning glance. He wants to get back to making his point. "Only those who have evolved to the point of hungering freedom are our kind as you say."

"And how many of your kind are there exactly?" Damian asks.

"I could say there are many, but that would be a lie. I didn't come here to lie. I can say the number is growing as word of the Queen spreads."

"Yet," Damian persists, "despite low numbers you sound extremely confident."

"Any confidence is extreme in this world." Wudak seems to be losing patience for the first time. "Do you want the aliens or not?"

"For all we know, you are setting a trap for us," Damian says.

"And why would I do that? Why wouldn't I have attacked you here with all my forces when you least expected it? I've known for weeks about your location. Why would

I risk my own hide dropping my weapons at your feet? Why wouldn't I lead my entire Regiment here?"

"He is telling the truth," Gritu adds as if his corroboration could make all the difference in the world.

"You are scared of Freya's receptor, that's why," Damian says to Wudak.

"There are ways around the receptor," Wudak says. "While she doesn't understand it, it can always be taken from her. It would probably take many Sliman lives, but it can be done. There are a few Lagerians left that can handle their receptors adequately. They could be brought in. The only reason it hasn't been done is because they don't know where you are."

"You still haven't given me a shred of evidence," Damian says.

"Fine, don't believe me, just let us take you to the alien convoy," Wudak says. "We're at your mercy. Keep us tethered. You can kill us on the spot if what we have said is not true."

"You see, there's a problem with that. It's only worth killing you if we can go on living after you're dead," Damian says.

"Don't you trust in your skills at all? Each one of you is special, we know that. You can sense danger. Don't you have faith in Freya's power? I do. That's why I'm here."

"Which one is it? Is she invincible or not?"

"Against eight Sliman and three aliens, she is. With us, she is."

Damian laughs but the laughter is short and unconvincing. He turns to me. "What do you think?"

"I think he's telling the truth," I say and I'm not even sure why. I wish Daphne was here. She would have known whether the Sliman are sincere or not. Her psychic powers would have penetrated through the deepest connections in their brains.

I kneel behind Wudak and, ignoring Damian's protests, untie the knots binding the Sliman Commander's wrists. "Don't make me regret this," I say as the rope falls away. "I know how to use the receptor. Maybe not in a perfect way, but I can make a mess of you."

Wudak extends one hand to invite Pip over.

"Freya?" Damian hisses, but I raise a hand to silence him.

To everyone's astonishment, Pip approaches Wudak without hesitation. The contrast between the two is striking—the tiny human girl and the massive mutant warrior.

Wudak places his palm gently over Pip's face. His eyes dim as though focusing inward. "You are restored," he says. "You are in the present. You are whole."

Wudak lets his hand drop. Pip looks exactly the same as before. Then, to our collective surprise, she smiles at Wudak—a genuine smile that transforms her face into something almost radiant.

I step toward her cautiously. "Pip, are you okay?"

She nods. "Freya, you are beautiful."

I laugh as I pull her into a tight embrace. When I release her, I turn to Wudak who watches us with an unreadable expression. "What was that? What did you do to her?"

"Just hypnosis to ease the neural recalibration sequence," Wudak says. "A select few among us were trained to perfect that capability." He turns back to Pip. "Apologies for the necessity to implement selective neural suppression on your cognitive structures." He pauses, nostrils flaring. "Being able to talk could have activated the memories I blocked—memories that could have caused you psychological anguish without us here to help stabilize your neural pathways. It will take some time for full restoration, but all your memories will return."

Boy... Judging by the look on Pip's face, Wudak might as well have been speaking in hieroglyphs.

❖

DAMIAN CATCHES UP WITH me on my way to find Finn. The gathering darkness is broken only by the soft glow of my lantern and the silver gleam of the moon. The plan has been laid out and rehashed so many times I could recite it in my sleep—if sleep were possible with everything at stake. In the morning, the Sliman will lead us along hidden paths to the spaceship landing area. With any luck, this mission won't turn out to be a complete fiasco like the last time we attempted something similar.

"Are you sure about this?" Damian says, walking beside me like a shadow. The edge in his voice makes me feel uncomfortable.

"I'm not sure, but I don't want to keep running for the rest of my life."

However short that might be.

"I'm going to trust you on this," he says after a weighted pause. "Just don't let go of that receptor, and don't leave my side tomorrow. You stay close to me no matter what happens."

"It's part of the plan, I know." His concern is justified, but it grates on my already frayed nerves.

How drastically everything has shifted. I was told to stay behind with Doc last time, but now I have a central part alongside Damian, Finn and Nya. Scout and Tilly will stay at the camp with Pip to maintain base security. Theo, Zoe, Doc, Biscuit and Rabbit will function as our backup forces.

"Where are you going?" Damian asks, tracking my movement with that protective focus of his.

"I'm looking for Finn."

His eyes narrow. "It's late, you should rest."

"Right, Damian, as if I can sleep."

He nods once, sliding his hands into his pockets. As he turns to go, a strange pang twists in my stomach. I can't shake the feeling that I owe him. Big time.

"Damian, wait," I call after him. "I know I've said it many times already, but I'm grateful to you for so many things. I appreciate how you try to keep an eye on me without being too meddlesome. We've come a long way, haven't we?"

He pauses, his broad shoulders silhouetted against the night sky. "Just don't let your guard down," he says, but I know he has a million things going through his mind. The responsibility he carries weighs on him even more now with the Sliman among us. The smallest mistake could cost us our lives.

I hold his hand in mine for a moment before heading to Finn's tent. I find him there with Rabbit who is fidgety as usual, pacing around Finn, fingers tapping against his thigh, eyes darting to every corner. Rabbit has never been good at hiding excitement, fear or any other intense emotion.

"Pip's with Scout and Tilly, Rabbit," I say. "Can you check on her for me?"

"Why? If she's with Scout and Tilly, she's perfectly fine. *I* won't be fine though if I go there. All that chattering and blabbering and gossiping. Now that Pip's verbal, they'll want to make up for lost time. No, thank you. I'd rather—"

"Rabbit!" I cut him short.

"Oh," he says as he finally catches on. "Right, I'll go check on her."

As his footsteps fade, Finn shakes his head. "Well, that was subtle."

"He was driving me crazy with all his bouncing around."

"No, he wasn't. You just want me all to yourself," Finn jokes.

"Yeah, that too."

I let my body drop to the floor like a heavy sack of rocks and pull my knees to my chin. I feel drained. Finn sits down beside me, our shoulders touching. I feel safe and cozy with him like I always have. The tragedy with Daphne, our quarrels, my fears—none of it has been able to break our bond. Finn and I are as close as ever. Our friendship has recovered, probably mostly because of him.

Finn the loyal. Finn the true. The place he has reserved for me in his heart will always be there. I know this now.

"It's happening," I say. "Again."

"So it is. And this time you're welcoming it."

"I am. It's necessary."

"Let's hope your instincts are better than mine," he says. Then he hurries to add, "They are. You have great instincts. I should listen to you more."

I nudge his shoulder with mine. "Don't take that resigned attitude with me, Finn. You're nothing but a blessing to me, to the Saviors, to this entire planet."

He smiles. "The planet might be a stretch, but thanks."

The proximity to Finn brings my guard down once again. It's easy to allow melancholy to creep in when warmth dissolves tension—Finn's warmth. I could use even more of it.

"I feel like a hypocrite," I say.

"Why? What have you done now?"

"Nothing, Finn! I need you to be on my side right now."

He sighs. "What's eating at you, Tick?"

I stare at my hands. "What the Sliman said about my other sister... I can't shake it. I don't know why it weighs on me so much. She's not the only child to have vanished from the plantations. It happens every day, we know that. So why does it matter more when it's my sister? Everyone's lost someone. You had a sister, too. At least I got Pip back, which is more than anyone else can say. I have no right to complain."

Finn takes my hand, tracing circles on my palm with his thumb. "It's not a competition, Freya. Grief doesn't work that way. You're allowed to hurt, to be vulnerable, to deal with your losses however you need to."

He pulls me closer, my head resting against his shoulder, and we stay that way for a while. I like it. Outside the night birds sing their beautiful cries of loneliness.

"I should go get Pip," I say, fighting every cell in my body. "It's getting late and tomorrow..." I kiss his cheek before I get up.

"Tick," he says, "everything will go as planned. We'll strike our first real victory."

I nod with a half-smile. "The receptor will make sure of that."

"Whatever happens," Finn says, "I love you, Freya. Never forget that."

"Yeah, me too," I say, feeling his words in my blood. I do my best to slip out of the tent as fast as possible.

CHAPTER 4

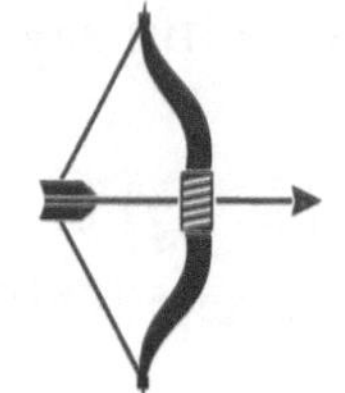

Dust and leaves fly up in the air behind Rabbit's feet as he runs back to us at full speed. He can run without making noise. His feet produce no audible signals. It's as if they don't even touch the ground. Rabbit running is a thing of wonder.

"They're on their way," he says. "I spotted the convoy. Five miles out. They're moving slowly. They should be here in ten minutes, maybe twelve."

Damian nods and unlocks his pulse gun. Finn does the same. Nya caresses her shock bow. I squeeze my fingers around the sensory receptor. Wudak has instructed me how to use it to create an invisible shield around us, a shield that will prevent even the alien sensors from locating us when they get close.

Creating the shield felt strange at first. My fingers had pins and needles and my vision got blurry, but now I can hold the shield in place without too much effort. The trick will be to switch from a defense mode to an attack mode within a split second. As soon as Wudak gives the sign, I'll have to let the shield down and build up an energy blast. I've never done this, but Wudak is confident I will pull it off. There's so much I have yet to learn.

The Sliman cannot help us in the fight. They cannot be seen. They cannot leave any trace behind. Their presence cannot be suspected, or it will be the end of them. They will remain hidden in the trees, hoping not to be picked up by the alien sensors among the commotion that the attack will surely create.

The convoy sensors can, in theory, send signals to the plantation network and that is our biggest fear. Theo doesn't have access to the satellite coordinates anymore and so he cannot block them.

Biscuit, Theo, Zoe and Doc have climbed onto the branches of two huge oak trees. They are scanning the area for the first visible signs of the convoy. My job will be to immobilize the aliens with the receptor before they have time to reach for theirs. It is more than likely they will carry at least one sensory receptor among them. I will have to act fast to prepare the terrain for Damian, Finn and Nya who will attack the Sliman guards head on once the aliens are under my control. Theo, Zoe, Doc and Biscuit will cover us with their pulse guns from above.

"Rabbit, tie all three Sliman up and stay close to them.

You can shoot them on the spot if they so much as move a finger," Damian says.

"Hang on," I say. "Damian, I need Wudak. You can't just have him tied up. I need his guidance."

"He doesn't need his hands for that, does he?"

"I can't believe you sometimes."

"I'm not changing my mind, Freya. End of the conversation."

Rabbit looks confused. He has no idea what to do until Damian repeats the order. Rabbit quickly ties Malzod and Gritu but hesitates with Wudak. Damian takes the rope from Rabbit and ties Wudak's hands behind his back.

"You can stay close to Freya until the convoy is here and she switches on her energy," he tells Wudak abruptly before he leaves to talk with Finn and Nya.

"I'd be careful with that one if I were you," Wudak says.

"What do you mean?" I say, quite astounded.

"He's after you. And not in a way that would make sense in human terms."

"The only thing that doesn't make sense is your words," I whisper.

"I wish I could reveal more. As it is, I can only promise to protect you."

My head starts spinning and my focus diminishes. That's no way to go into battle.

"Steady there," Wudak says, sensing my frustration.

"Do not pay attention to my ramblings. Like I said, I don't understand human vulnerability all that well."

"On the contrary, I think you understand us quite well. I think you're trying to create problems for us. Making us suspicious of each other."

"Forgive my insolence, it will not happen again," Wudak promises, avoiding my eyes.

All thoughts are erased from my mind as Biscuit gives the sign. He sees them. The convoy is approaching. We all move to take our positions.

The seconds go by with remarkable sluggishness, dragging their feet inside my ears with a ticking sound. Every beat of my heart lasts an eternity.

I hear the sound of the alien vehicle. It moves slowly to keep pace with the Sliman who are on foot. They might as well be a brigade of marching elephants in metal boots.

Wudak bumps me gently with his shoulder. "It's time, dear Freya," he says. "I will count to three and then you will let the shield fall and you'll bring your blasting energy back. Allow your brain to be fluid in its commands. Do not strain yourself."

I nod and he starts counting.

"One."

Damian's right behind me.

"Two."

Finn and Nya on each side.

"Three."

I place the receptor in front of my face and gently blow at it. My breath is visible as it touches the small screen on the device. Immediately, the energy switches and I jump out of the trees and right in front of the convoy. The two Sliman guards that lead the way are caught unawares and waste valuable seconds before reacting.

It's all I need. My receptor's energy field slams the alien vehicle and tears off its roof. At the same time, the aliens are engulfed in a blue mist that keeps them immobilized. Their breathing becomes labored and they have to focus their entire being on that simple function.

Simultaneously, Damian falls over the two leading guards. He grabs them by their necks and crashes them with a ferociousness that I have not seen in him before. Their lifeless bodies fall to the ground.

Finn and Nya attack the remaining six Sliman, Finn from the left and Nya from the right, in an avalanche of pulse gun blasts coming from the trees. Two more Sliman go down. Damian steps in front of me and walks to the open vehicle that holds the three stunned aliens inside.

"You're free," he tells me as he pounces down on the aliens with all his force.

I stare at him in horror, unable to reconcile the violence of his assault with the gentleness I have seen in him. I realize that he doesn't just want to kill the aliens, he wants them to suffer a bit first. He wants them to know they are at his mercy. That is why he instructed me not to kill them with the receptor. It was not to avoid having the vehicle explode on us like he said. It was so that he could finish the job himself.

I wake from my trance when I hear Nya scream. The eight Sliman are all dead or badly wounded but a ninth Sliman has appeared out of nowhere. He has thrown a knife at Nya's thigh. I turn the receptor on him, but Finn reacts faster and shoots the Sliman dead. Doc climbs down the tree as fast as he can and rushes to Nya's side. Her thigh is bleeding. The knife is still inside her flesh. Doc examines the wound and places a gauze around the knife before he pulls it out.

"No punctured arteries and the knife's not magnetic," he says, relieved.

My hands tremble and I feel weak in my stomach.

"Are you okay, Freya?" Finn says. "You look so pale."

"I'm fine, don't worry about me."

Finn calls Zoe and Theo to check out the surrounding area, guns in hand.

I look to Damian. My heart freezes. He lifts his face to the sky. His hands and shirt are covered in blood, and his features are hardened. In his hands, he holds the two sensors he has found in the vehicle. They are bloodied as well.

He looks like a primitive god, a warrior king. I turn my face away in shock. Maybe I am too naïve. Maybe he's right about this as well. You can't win a war with kindness.

I rub my hands together. They feel clammy and cold. I always get cold when I get a bad feeling. I sense a shadow behind me and when I turn, I come face to face with Wudak. He looks down on me silently.

"I'm not that interesting, stop staring at me," I blurt out, but he doesn't respond. I take a look at Nya. Doc has cleaned and bandaged her wound. Biscuit gives her water and a slice of bread.

"Is she okay?" I ask.

"She's fine," Doc says. "She'll recover quickly."

I nod and I take off into the woods looking for a moment alone. A moment to pull myself together. To take in all that has just happened.

We have won, we've killed three alien invaders for the first time, and we have made a statement. Wudak's word was good. He has proven that he can be trusted to some extent. I wish he'd never stare at me that way again though. His deep green eyes are so penetrating, I feel like he could expose my soul. I'm afraid he can sense that I somehow failed myself during the fight, that my thoughts took over and, for a few moments, I was useless and looking at things from a distance.

I need to grow thicker skin, maybe become more like the Sliman fighters who can literally make their skin thicker when it's too cold, or they're in a fight or underwater.

Most of all, I need to examine my feelings for Damian.

I need to see why I spend so much energy trying to figure him out.

I take a deep breath, tap the receptor in my pocket to make sure it's there and decide to go back.

Before I take two steps, Damian approaches me with long strides. It's the last thing I need right now.

"You can't run off like that," he says and before I know what's going on, he lifts me up and hides his face in my hair. "That felt good back there, didn't it? We make a good team."

"Put me down," I say, but his lips are on mine already. I feel paralyzed, unable to push him away, and this time I can't blame it on overwhelming grief. I've grown closer to him over the past couple of months. I've come to like him and trust him. I even like it when he kisses me. But being with him is not an option for so many different reasons.

"Put me down," I repeat as I pull away.

He does so but a moment later he pulls me in his arms and kisses my neck. His breath is warm and sweet and his tenderness takes me by surprise. I have to be careful or this won't end well.

"What the hell are you doing?" I say. "You can't just grab people and kiss them whenever you feel like it."

He turns his head left then right to show his bewilderment. "People? What does that mean? I don't kiss people. I kissed *you*. And you kissed me back."

"This is the part where you're supposed to apologize."

"Don't hold your breath."

"You make me so furious sometimes. You can never do that again, do you hear me?"

"Sure, if that's what you want."

"Yes, that is what I want."

"Fine."

"Let's get back. I can't believe we're arguing about such stupidities in the middle of nowhere while our lives and the lives of our friends could still be in danger. Do you have any idea how inappropriate this is?" I keep going on about how we could jeopardize everything by being careless, how we should put the common good first. I keep talking so I won't hear my own thoughts.

"You will grow up one day," is the only thing he says in response. He speeds up his pace and leaves me behind.

⬥

PIP COMES RUNNING WHEN we return to the camp late in the evening. "You're all safe," she says, clapping her hands together.

Finn winks at her. "Of course we are, what did you think? We have superpowers, remember?"

Tilly's eyes widen as she spots the bloodied bandage on Nya's leg. "Nya, what happened?"

"A little souvenir," Nya says, smiling. "So I remember the day I killed two freaky Slimies."

Gritu cringes at this. "I'm not slimy."

Nya offers him one of her coldest smiles. "Of course not," she says, rolling her eyes.

Scout, Tilly and Pip can't help but laugh, but they stop when Wudak and Damian come in last. The seriousness on their faces cools the celebratory mood.

Damian waits until we've all gathered at the cave entrance before speaking. "The Sliman have given signs of trustworthiness. They can stay tonight. Unarmed but guarded." He turns to Wudak, "You understand that I cannot let you walk freely about the camp. From now on, you will need to notify us of your visits in advance."

"It's not a problem," Wudak says. "We do not plan to visit again."

"We need details of the fight," Tilly interrupts.

Scout nods eagerly. "How did it all go down?"

"We'll give you all the details," Damian says with a smile, "while we enjoy our victory feast."

"Finally, something worth living for," Biscuit says, patting his stomach.

Rabbit perks up. "I'll get the dishes out."

"We're not done," Damian says to Wudak as most of the Saviors disperse to prepare for the celebration. Only Theo and I still linger outside.

"No, we are not," Wudak agrees.

"What do you mean you're not visiting again? I thought your gran plan was to train Freya, to protect her."

Wudak closes in on Damian, their faces inches apart. They look like giant bulls about to ram each other. "We're taking her with us."

Damian laughs in his face. "So you do have a sense of humor," he says then turns to me. "Did you hear that, Freya? Pack your bags."

"I just might and there's nothing you can do about it," I snap back just to provoke him. I don't know what's wrong with me.

He stares at me a long while and I can see murder on his face. He decides to drop it. "I'll go get cleaned up," he says.

Theo shakes his head before following Damian. He's sad. He doesn't understand. He's disappointed in me. I can feel it. There's no room for the old, reactionary Freya anymore.

Wudak grabs my arm, and I jerk it away instinctively as fast as I can.

"What are you doing?" I say.

"If you never trust me but once, let this be the time," he whispers to me. "Stay far away from him."

CHAPTER 5

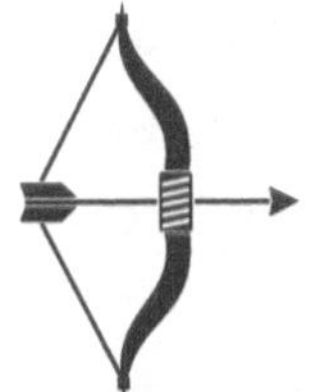

IN A SINGLE MOMENT everything we ever wished for might be taken away from us. In a dark corner of the universe, a genetic mix might be boiled in a laboratory to destroy the world as we know it. Things that we thought held the most importance for us—family, love, possessions, education—would become irrelevant then and we'd find ourselves running away from the flames just to stay alive for a few more days, hours, minutes.

That's what happened to the citizens of this world when the first alien invading ships arrived and began to bomb every major city in the world. That's how dreams turned into ruins and that's how intelligence turned itself inside out and concentrated its entire purpose on finding a way to survive.

It's a sad story and an even sadder lesson. But it is also the motivation a broken soul needs in order to invent a new world. To be reborn like the bird Phoenix out of ashes and tears.

The night has been full of wonders. The three Sliman have been ecstatic over Biscuit's culinary talents, and he has accepted their exaggerated compliments with a solemnity that borders on the absurd.

Pip has revealed a new side to her, a side that's wise and thoughtful and consistent with the wonderful sweetness and politeness we saw in her from the beginning. She has asked me not to grieve over the loss of our sister but try and remember her instead. Try and keep her alive in our memories. We have decided to ask all the girls to join us in a reunion and get to talk about those we've lost, about us, about the future and our hopes for it.

I wish I could take Pip to the library but it's not safe anymore. All I can do is relate my favorite stories to her, explain the world as I have understood it through my readings and conversations with the rest of the Saviors, especially Finn.

I remember the day I took my little sisters out in the woods surrounding the breeding village to show them how to pick mushrooms that were safe to eat. It was only a few days before my harvesting, and I knew we didn't have much time. I was seven and Pip was barely two. Our sister was four. We called her Four. We all called each other by our age in the village, changing names every year. We didn't know anything else.

My brother had done the same thing for me days before he was harvested. He showed me how to pick mushrooms, how to pull dandelions out of the ground without breaking them, and how to find colorful bird eggs.

I wanted to do the same for my sisters, but they were too young and all they wanted to do was play. I threw my rope around a branch to make a swing, and we pushed each other for a long time. We played hide and seek, and we rolled down a slope. When we returned to the hut, my mother gave us soup and apples. We all slept together on the floor that night, and I can still feel the girls' soft breathing in my ears.

It's getting really late. There are more than a few yawns in the company, but nobody feels like going to bed. The excitement of the day has not died down yet. We sit around a bonfire with the Sliman sitting a bit further away. I have to turn my head to see them. They look out of place but do their best not to draw attention to themselves.

Our faces take on a strange orange hue as the fire reflects on them. The stories we tell make our skin crawl. We talk about werewolves and vampires, about zombies and ogres that are after human flesh. Scary stories all, but our real lives are more frightening than anything we could conjure. Yet, I get a creepy feeling I can't shake and so do most of the other girls. Not Nya though, she's enjoying the stories and wants to hear more.

"Who would win in a hand-to-hand combat?" she asks. "A vampire or a werewolf?"

"A vampire," Rabbit says. "There's no question about it."

"Werewolves have their own tricks up their sleeves and they're super-strong. They could win," Scout says.

"Nine out of ten times a vampire would win," Biscuit says.

"Ten out of ten times a Sliman would win," Malzod says. It's the first time we've heard him say anything at all. So far, he's just listened and nodded. Maybe he likes our stories.

"Does today count?" Nya says to prod him.

Malzod crosses his arms and retreats into silence again. It's possible that he is not pleased with what happened today. Maybe if it were up to him, no Sliman would have been sacrificed. Maybe he thinks there should have been a better way to prove their loyalty to us. I know that's what I'd think in his shoes anyway.

Finn and Theo play a game of chess with a set that I have helped make, carving the pawns out of pieces of wood until my fingers blistered. As always, the game hangs in perfect balance and can go either way. They are both equally skilled at chess.

"So, Tick," Damian whispers as he moves closer to me, "do you think your boyfriend will win this time?"

My head snaps left and right to make sure nobody has

heard him. "What is the matter with you?" I hiss under my breath.

He shrugs. "What did I do this time, Tick?"

"Don't ever call me that again."

"Is that one more of your orders?"

"Yes. Now leave me alone."

He obeys for now and retreats to his spot between Doc and Zoe. Across the fire, Pip's laughter rings out as she sits with Tilly and Scout. Rabbit's right, these three have formed a circle of friendship all their own. A *triangle* of friendship, in Rabbit's words.

I pull at my fingers one by one until they crack. Then, as my frustration overpowers me, I call Pip over.

"Pip," I whisper, "you don't have to tell people everything you know."

Pip is confused. "What do you mean, Freya?"

"I mean like the other day when you told Damian why Finn called me Tick. That was something private between Finn and me, and you shouldn't have shared it with Damian."

Now Pip is even more confused. "Why?" she says. "Aren't we all a family here?"

"Yes, we are. But even families have secrets. Especially families."

"I'm sorry, Freya. I have so much to learn."

My cheeks go red with shame. *What am I doing?* "Oh, Pip, no, you don't. I'm sorry, you didn't do anything wrong." I reach for her hand. How could I accuse Pip of anything? She's the kindest, brightest person, and she has helped me become a better person, too.

Oh, this is pointless. I push myself to my feet, ready to escape to my tent. I need space to sort through the chaos in my head, to try and put things in order.

"Freya, wait." Zoe catches my arm before I can slip away. "I have a question for you."

"What is it?"

"That Sliman, Wudak," she starts, lowering her voice. "He's had his eyes on you all night. Are you sure he can be trusted?"

"You mean he's been watching me?"

"Like a hawk. Every time your face is turned away, he watches you. Every time you close your eyes, he watches you. Every time you talk, his eyes are on you." She leans closer. "I think that's why he chose to sit behind you. So that he could watch you without you knowing."

"I caught him looking at me a couple of times," I admit. "I just didn't realize it was constant."

"He's making me nervous," Zoe says. "Keep an eye on him."

"I will. But, honestly, can I tell you something? Something that you may not repeat?"

Zoe nods.

"I think he somehow cares for me. I don't know why, but I think all he wants to do is watch over me."

Zoe is not convinced. "If Daphne were here, she'd see right through him."

"I know. For now, all I have to go by is my instinct."

So, one more thing to worry about, I think as I trudge toward my tent. I step in and almost let a scream out. There's a shadow inside the tent, a human shape where there shouldn't be one. As my initial shock fades, I realize it's Damian.

"What on earth, Damian?" I say, fumbling to light a candle. "When did you get here?"

"A couple minutes before you."

"While I was talking to Zoe."

"Yes."

"What do you want now?" My tone is irritated and abrupt, but it doesn't seem to bother him. He's getting used to it. He might even welcome the challenge. I have created a nightmare.

"I don't like the way we've been acting," he says. "I came to apologize. Let's start all over."

"Again?"

"Yes, again. Why not?"

"Okay, sure. But you have to promise, no more kissing and no more *Tick* jokes for you."

He doesn't like where this is going. It remains to be seen whether what he's just said about turning over a new leaf is genuine or just another strategy. I have to push him a little if I am to know if I can trust his words.

"Are you sure that's what you want?" is all he says in the end.

I nod. What can I say to him? That I don't know what I want? That I am confused beyond belief? To him that would sound encouraging, and I don't want to do that.

"Don't you want to see if this could work, Freya?"

"I don't need to see. I know it wouldn't work. And if you were being honest with yourself, you'd know it too. We're not compatible in any sense of the word. We don't belong together, Damian. Besides, there's so much at stake. This is hardly the time."

He sits down on my bed, and I think I've gotten through to him to some extent. I don't see any red on his face, or any throbbing veins at his temples, and he hasn't attempted to grab me or steal another kiss.

"You don't owe Finn any loyalty," he says, and just like that, the moment shatters.

"It's not about that, Damian."

"As a matter of fact, you shouldn't trust him blindly. He's not as spotless as you think."

I spoke too soon. He hasn't given up. He doesn't know how to lose. He needs to be in control all the time, and I cannot afford to forget that.

"Just go, Damian. Get out."

"He will lie to you. Again and again. He's really good at it."

"Get out already!"

"How can you trust a guy who risks the lives of his companions on a whim?"

"And how can I trust a guy who badmouths his friends behind their backs? Even Wudak told me to be careful with you."

"Oh, so you're going to take the word of a Sliman over mine?"

"I don't know if you've noticed, but this isn't going according to your plan. I'm getting more pissed at you by the second."

He does his best to compose himself. "I'm sorry," he says with practiced control. "I will do my best not to upset you again."

He steps out, ducking through the tent flap, and I should feel relieved, but I don't. Instead, I just feel an ocean of emptiness. I lie back in my small tent, tired and alone.

CHAPTER 6

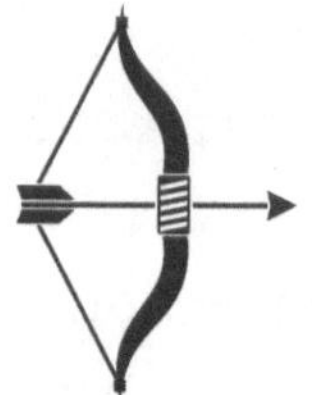

THE RUSH OF RUNNING water in the distance... the heavy scent of lilies in bloom... but the darkness is absolute, pressing against my eyelids. Then the ground shakes violently and I reach out blindly for an anchor... something... anything to steady myself...

A hand... a hand I desperately need to trust. I hold on tight, but the hand quivers like a frantic bird and I lose my balance. I plunge into a void and I hear my name repeated like an echo over and over.

I gasp as my eyes snap open. The sudden light stabs at my retinas, and I blink, wincing.

Finn leans over me, his brow furrowed with concern.

I rub my eyes. "What's going on?"

"It's late, you slept in." He sounds almost apologetic.

I sit up and scan my surroundings. The tent is neatly organized—Pip's bed is meticulously made, the small table scrubbed clean and my water bottle filled to the brim, waiting.

"Where's Pip?"

"She's up already. Said she didn't have the heart to wake you."

"I didn't sleep well." The fragments of my dream cling to me like cobwebs. "Sorry, I had no idea it was this late."

"The Sliman are leaving. They need to speak with you before they go."

"You mean they're waiting for me?"

Finn nods.

Because my life wasn't complicated enough already. "Okay, give me a second and I'll be ready."

I make a move to get out of bed, then freeze. Blood rushes to my face. *Damn.* I'm naked. The night felt so oppressively hot, the air so thick, that I couldn't tolerate anything on me.

"Turn the other way," I order Finn, pulling the thin blanket higher.

"What?" he says, but then he gets it. "Right, I'll wait outside."

You can do this, I tell myself as I jump out of bed and yank on my old pants and shirt. The fabric is worn thin at the knees and elbows. It's been months since the last time I found anything new to wear. Months since I've been to Lost Town.

I brush my hair with quick, long strokes. I'll have to ask

Nya, who has a surprisingly steady hand with scissors, to give me a haircut soon.

I gulp down some water and splash the rest over my face. I pat myself dry with a towel and hesitate for a moment before applying some of Zoe's precious face cream, the one she swears will make your skin glow *like you've slept like a baby.*

I pause, fingers on my cheeks. What am I even doing? Why do I suddenly care about appearance?

Finn tucks his touchpad into his pocket when I step out. We walk in silence to Damian's tent—the largest in the camp, of course. It could easily fit all of us and then some. I notice that besides Damian and the Sliman, only Zoe, Doc and Theo are present. This is a meeting of what we jokingly call *the oldest six* then. Nya is only months younger than Theo, but she avoids these inner circle meetings like a festering wound. "I'd rather practice than talk," is her standard excuse and Damian has given up trying to convince her otherwise.

The Sliman sit cross-legged on the floor but rise in unnerving unison when they see me, like I'm some kind of general leading their troops. Or a queen. Isn't that what they called me?

"Are you sick?" Wudak says, his eyes scanning my face with uncomfortable intensity.

"No, what gave you that idea?"

"You're late. We've waited for you for over an hour."

"I'm sorry, I just slept in."

Just what they needed to hear. Their queen can't even drag herself out of bed on time.

We all settle down on the floor—six Saviors versus three Sliman. That's unprecedented, to say the least.

"We have to go," Wudak begins. "We have to be back at our posts by tonight. Our allies in the Regiment can only cover for us until then. We're supposed to be on a scouting mission this whole time."

It hits me that they're risking their lives just by being here, and I've made them wait needlessly.

"Yesterday, you said you wouldn't return," I say, cutting to the chase to speed things up.

"We *will* come back," Wudak says. "For you. We'll take you to a safe place beyond Lagerian reach, a shielded location where the drones can't find you."

Um, what? "I don't think that's possible. I can't leave my friends behind. And frankly, I don't trust you enough to hand over my life."

"Perhaps if we explain to you what you *are*, you will understand your importance," Wudak says.

I nod, bracing myself. Zoe pats my shoulder, a small, comforting gesture that does little to soothe my nerves. We both know this won't be pleasant.

"The aliens... the Lagerians... have altered your DNA, and that goes for all of you," Wudak starts. "Before you were even born. It's the reason you possess these unique strengths, the abilities that set you apart. Each of you is the result of a different experiment, a distinct variation in the genetic code."

"As are we," Gritu adds.

"We have suspected as much," Doc says, nodding. "The outliers of human evolution."

"Not all experiments are successful," Wudak goes on. "Most children show no special abilities, and some children fall ill and die as their bodies reject the alterations. A few, like the twelve of you, thrive and grow to become enhanced humans."

"But why?" Doc asks, his brow furrowed. "Why would they do this?"

"Because they're after one particular mutation," Wudak says as he glances at me.

"Freya's," Finn says.

"Yes, Freya's," Wudak confirms, his eyes drilling into me. "As far as we know, you are the only one. The culmination of their experiments."

"So, they want me to use the receptors for them?" I ask, still struggling to take all this information in. "Do they want to experiment more on me, now that they can't fully control the receptors themselves? Cut me open, poke around, see what I can *do*?"

"No, that's not... the full picture."

"Then what *is* it?"

The next words seem caught in Wudak's throat. He

shakes his head and looks to his companions for validation, seeking permission to unleash the devastating truth he's been holding back. "Freya, you are an alien bride."

"What in the *hell* does that mean?" Finn says.

"It means her genetic makeup is compatible with that of the Lagerians," Doc says out of breath.

The implications... No, I don't want to think of the implications.

"None of this makes sense," I say. "Are you telling me that I'm not even human?"

"You are human, but you have mutated genes. The genotype of your cells includes certain attributes that are needed for..."

"Needed for what?" Zoe presses.

I start feeling nauseous. I'm not sure I want to hear what's coming next. My body is screaming for me to run, to block out the hideous truth.

Wudak clears his throat. "The Lagerians have been in decline for decades. You have witnessed it first-hand—their frailty, their dependence on us. They are decaying fast... fading. Only a few thousand remain as far as we know. Their superior technology and medical advancements are keeping them alive, but for how long? All of them are male now. The females have all died, wiped out by some catastrophic genetic mutation that hit their gender first. The aliens can no longer procreate. Not without a compatible host capable of carrying their embryos to term and save their species from extinction."

My blood freezes in an instant. "They want me to carry their embryos?" I can't believe what I'm hearing. There has to be a mistake. This can't be real.

"Yes. They can clone their cells and create embryos, but they cannot have the embryos grow in an artificial environment. The process always fails. They need a living host, which is where you come in. Your nervous and immune systems, your chromosomes... something within your genetic code I don't fully understand makes you uniquely suited. You are the missing piece they've been waiting for all this time."

It slowly begins to dawn on me. "That's why they didn't want to risk killing me."

"Kill you? They don't want to kill you. They have been trying to create you for many years. They are getting old. You are the only hope for their species."

"They just want to use me for breeding?"

"Yes. And now that they know that it can be done, they will do it again and again. All they need is your sequential number, so they know what specimen you are, then will replicate it. They will mutate every little girl the same way. Most of them will die. If we hadn't erased your data, they would already know."

I instinctively reach for the tattooed number on the back of my neck. This is far worse than anything I could have imagined.

"Do you understand how important it is that you stay safe?" Wudak asks. "A lot of children will suffer if you're caught, not just you."

"And those creatures will cover your Earth like a plague," Gritu says. "It will be their planet, and then they will eliminate human and Sliman alike."

"If they never find you, they will eventually die out," Wudak says. "They left their planet because they thought the atmosphere was what was weakening them; because they destroyed it somehow. But now every planet they invade rejects them in the end. They're running out of time."

My mind is made up. "Where are you going to take me?"

"We have an underground base. You can stay there until you're strong enough to fight them. We'll train you, we'll show you what you can do with the sensory receptor device. We'll serve you and we'll be loyal to you throughout this entire war. In exchange, we want our freedom and Omicron 5."

It's a fair request. Between Doc and me, we could probably do it.

"We don't get separated," Damian says. "The Saviors stay together."

"We understand. You can all join us," Wudak says with his head lowered. "You will be safe and you can enjoy all that we have to offer."

THE DECISION IS MADE—WE'LL go with our new Sliman allies. When they return in two days, they will lead us to their underground base. We'll have to travel through our very own woods to get there. It will be a journey not only into an uncertain future but also a haunting trip through our past.

Finn sits beside me on the riverbank. Our feet are dipped in the cool, flowing water. It's a small river, more like a creek really, but there's plenty of tiny fish darting around our ankles and tickling our toes as they swim downstream.

Our world... a world we're leaving behind.

"I don't know how I'm going to tell Shy Boy that we're leaving," I say.

"He will be fine," Finn says. "He'll spend more time with his own kind. It's what's best for him."

"Pip will miss him."

"We're doing this for him, too. For every living thing that ever had to suffer at the hands of the aliens."

I kick my feet in the water, disrupting the peaceful surface. The cool spray splashes against our legs.

"Do you see me differently now?" I ask, avoiding his eyes.

"Differently how?"

"Now that you know I'm part alien."

"You silly girl." He reaches out and pulls me into a hug. "We all are."

I look up at him, at his dark hair, his bluish-green eyes and the curve of his soft lips, and the love I feel for him almost takes my breath away. I could kiss him, lean all the way into our connection, but the timing feels impossibly wrong—too late for some carefree teenage romance, or maybe too terrifyingly soon for something real.

The truth is, I don't know what Finn wants. I could ask him, but I'm paralyzed by the fear of losing what we already have, the fear of change, of new complications, of rejection.

Yet, deep down, like the river flowing forward, it feels like Finn and I ought to end up together. Everyone seems to think so, at least according to Tilly and her relentless matchmaking efforts. We know each other so well, share so much love and trust, and there have been fleeting moments, electric sparks, when I felt him drawing closer. Moments when those same questions I have were about to form on his lips, but we're always interrupted by a friend, a foe, the universe, or one of us chickens out, retreating back into the comfortable safety of friendship.

Maybe it would be better to wait until the situation with the Sliman is sorted out, but I don't know if that even matters. Is there ever going to be an absolutely appropriate time for such a risky conversation? For risking everything on a single kiss?

Besides, according to the movies I watched at the Lost Town library, there's no need for clumsy conversations. A moment will arise, a convergence of fate and longing, that overwhelms us. Our lonely hearts will melt together into a kiss, soundtracked by soaring violins, and all our fears will magically vanish—or something equally improbable. So far, there are no signs that Finn is looking for that moment with me. Damian surely does. His signs have all the subtlety of a sledgehammer.

I pull my feet out of the water and escape Finn's embrace and his disarming charm.

"What's wrong?" he says.

"I told Pip I'd be back by now," I say as I put my boots on. "She wants me to help her practice her combat skills."

"I'll walk back with you."

"No. I want to walk alone. I need time to think. I haven't fully processed this... alien bride thing." That's not entirely true and I hate lying to Finn. The truth is I want to walk Damian out of my mind if I have to walk for three straight days.

Finn lies back on the riverbank with his arms folded behind his head and closes his eyes. I wonder what thoughts occupy his mind. Or maybe he's not thinking at all. Maybe he's connecting with the earth, the river, the roots of his very being as he's described it before. He is so peaceful and in touch with himself. I envy that quiet strength, that inner stillness I never seem to achieve.

I kneel down next to his right ear. "Finn, you're the man every girl dreams about in the old stories," I whisper out of the blue before I walk away.

CHAPTER 7

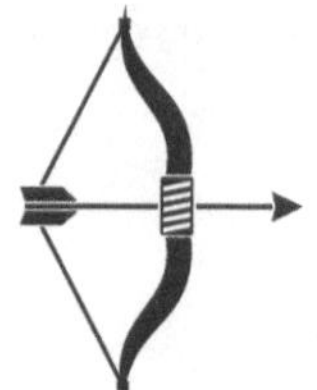

Tilly hands out vanilla, sugar and raspberry cookies from a woven straw basket. She's turned out to be quite the skilled baker since becoming Biscuit's apprentice.

It's late afternoon and the breeze gently rustles the tree branches overhead. We've gathered to honor the siblings we'll likely never see again. It was Pip's idea, and all the girls eagerly agreed to participate. For the past hour, we've been sharing memories about the ones we've lost, revealing details of our lives at the breeding villages for the first time.

Scout is the only one who grew up without siblings, but she had friends at the village that she misses. Tilly had two younger brothers that always caused trouble for her. Nya had an older brother, her confidant, and a younger sister she barely remembers. Zoe had three sisters, all of them older than her. She clings to the faintest glimmer of hope that they might still be alive, perhaps in another breeding village, but she knows the chances are slim. And even if she found them, would they recognize her?

We sit in the dappled shade of the fir trees, savoring our cookies, drawing out the pleasure of each bite. Nya has to keep her injured leg stretched out to let it heal. She makes loud, theatrical noises as she chews to demonstrate her appreciation. It's an obvious act, but it's fun to hear her try so hard.

Scout raises her hand, her eyes bright with mischief.

"Go on," says self-appointed moderator Zoe.

"Is it okay to gossip?" Scout says.

"What do you mean?" Zoe says. "Who can we gossip about? We're all here."

"I don't know... the guys maybe? Or the Sliman?" Scout says.

"Eww, I really don't want to talk about the Sliman," Tilly says. "They give me the creeps."

"We could gossip about ourselves," Pip offers.

"Gossip isn't gossip if the gossiped-about person is present during the gossiping," Nya says, her voice deadpan.

"What?" Pip says, staring at Nya confused.

"Ok, that's enough, Aristotle," Zoe says, rolling her eyes at Nya. "Scout, since it was your idea, you go first. I don't care what it's about, just start spilling."

I can't help but notice that Scout is a little too eager

about this gossiping session. She puts her entire body behind her words, practically spitting them out. "Biscuit has been visiting our tent *a lot* to talk to Tilly. And sometimes they *disappear* together."

"Hey!" Tilly protests, cheeks flushing. "That's not gossiping, that's telling!"

I roll my eyes. "Is that it?"

"Well, the way you say it, it's like you expected something earth-shattering," Scout scolds me.

"The way *I* see it, everybody knows about that already," I say with a fake yawn.

"What does everyone know, Freya?" Tilly asks, her face turning a vibrant red.

"That you and Biscuit are totally love birds," Nya jumps in.

"What's *that* supposed to mean?" Tilly says.

"Tilly," I say, "you can relax. We're happy for you. We're glad you have something cooking with Biscuit."

Everyone laughs and Tilly manages a smile, even as she blushes furiously. "Very funny, Tick," she says with a grin. "At least I'm not the one with a cute nickname."

Now it's my turn to blush. All the other girls are enjoying this gathering way more than Tilly and I.

"Neither of you has to be so secretive about it," Scout says. "I just thought you can save a lot of energy if you put it out in the open."

"It's okay to have secrets," Pip says. "Especially in a family."

Oh boy. What have I done to Pip? "I don't have any secrets," I say with a matter-of-fact tone. "You all know I'm the chosen alien bride. What else could possibly be worth hiding?"

I meant this as a joke, a way to deflect the attention, but judging from the girls' faces... *Not a joke.*

"And really," I go on, desperate to salvage the mood, "we shouldn't tease Tilly. She likes to be the one doing the teasing, remember?"

The girls manage weak smiles, but Pip still looks troubled about the *alien bride* part. I have to remember she's very new to the free world, so unfamiliar with casual banter. She takes everything literally, she hasn't been exposed to books or movies, and she lacks the years of shared experiences and endless fire-side conversations that have allowed us to navigate complex situations and emotional nuances.

"It's true, I do like to tease. But always in good spirit," Tilly says.

"You're probably one of the nicest people in the history of the world, Tilly," Zoe says. "You make everyone smile even when they're trying not to."

Tilly reaches a decision. "Okay, fine. I like Biscuit and I trust you girls with this information. Don't make me regret it."

"Finally," Scout says. "That's all I was hoping for. You don't have to play this weird hide-and-seek game with us, Tilly. We're on your side."

I think that's the end of the *love* conversation, but I'm wrong. It doesn't come from Pip as I feared. It comes from Tilly herself. "Maybe you would like to trust us with the same kind of information, Freya."

I shake my head in panic.

"Yes, it's about time," Scout chips in. "Tell us, Freya. *Everything.*"

"There's nothing to tell," I say, my voice rising. "We've talked about this, Tilly, exhaustively."

"I didn't believe you then and I don't believe you now," Tilly says with a pout.

"Do we have to spell it out for you?" Zoe teases.

"Zoe, come on, you too?" I scold her.

"Why not me? I can tease just as well as everyone else. Stop deflecting. Tell us all the juicy details."

I don't see a way out of this. Hell, I've watched them ambush alien convoys with more finesse than they're using right now to ambush me. "Are you done yet?"

"Hmm, let's see... no, not quite," Zoe says, tapping her chin. "Oh Romeo, Romeo, wherefore art thou, Romeo?"

Nya bends her face at that, and, surprisingly, jumps into the arena. "I think they are less Romeo and Juliet and more Heathcliff and Cathy."

I'm definitely not enjoying this. If they can't tell by

now, they're just dumb. Or maybe they *can* tell. And that's exactly what they want.

"Anthony and Cleopatra," Tilly suggests.

Pip, bless her heart, is totally confused, but adds, "Finn and Freya."

The aliens won't stand a chance with these girls after them.

Pip tugs on my sleeve. "What do they mean exactly, Freya? Didn't they know Finn is your best friend?"

"Of course, they know. They're just teasing... playing a game."

I know how to answer Pip, but not the others. If I truly defended myself, I'd sound ridiculous and pathetic. Should I even try? They could be right after all.

"Didn't all those people die miserable deaths?" I blurt out. It's the best I can do.

"I like Theo," Nya confesses out of nowhere.

Thank you, Nya. Her unexpected confession is a welcome distraction that draws the spotlight away from me in an instant.

"You like Theo?" Zoe asks, more than a little suspicious of Nya's declaration.

"I don't even know why. He's kind of cute, I guess," Nya says, shrugging, as she starts nibbling on a cookie.

"Now wait a moment, you can't just throw a thing like that and then act like it's the most normal thing in the world," Zoe says, nostrils flaring.

"Do you like him, too?" Nya says.

"That's not the point. Well, of course I like him, I care for him, but not like that. I just don't want you to make a fool out of him, Nya."

"Good. He's too young for you," Nya says through bouts of loud chewing.

Zoe is about to retaliate when we hear a rustling sound in the nearby trees. The sound stops almost immediately, but when it starts again, it has moved closer.

"What is that?" Tilly says.

"Shy Boy," Pip says. I realize it's the first time I've heard her say his name.

Zoe scans the tree line. "Your chimp?"

"He's not ours but yes," I say. I turn to Pip. "We have to say goodbye."

Pip nods. A sweet sorrow overtakes the smile on her face.

We excuse ourselves, leaving our friends behind to head toward the rustling sounds. We find Shy Boy sitting at the root of his favorite tree, the very tree where we first met him.

He looks up at us, his intelligent eyes filled with a mixture of curiosity and apprehension as if he's sensing our tension. We offer him cookies, and he chuckles at the sight of them. He eats quickly and when he's finished, he offers us a handful of berries.

"Yum, Shy Boy, where did you get these? These are so tasty," I say.

Pip's eyes shine with gratitude. "They are delicious."

Shy Boy cocks his head to one side, startled. He's never heard Pip talk before, not in full sentences, not intentionally. He walks around her sniffing the air, trying to figure out what's different about her. Then he bares his upper teeth in a wide grin, making some shrilling, affectionate sounds.

Pip laughs. "Stop going around in circles, you're making me dizzy."

Shy Boy settles onto the ground with a heavy thud, extending his arms. Pip climbs onto his lap, burying her face in his soft fur.

"We have to tell you something, Shy Boy," I say.

He looks up at me, his eyes filled with trust and affection, and my heart breaks. I don't know how I'm going to tell him that we're leaving, that we're probably never going to see him again. How do you explain goodbye to someone who doesn't understand *forever*?

"We have to go," Pip says.

"We won't be back for a very long time," I say. "Maybe never."

Shy Boy starts picking gently at Pip's hair.

"Shy Boy, you can't make this go away. Pip and I have to go. We'll be in danger if we stay. But you'll be safe here, with your friends, in the forest where you belong."

I speak slowly, looking into his eyes. Shy Boy can understand at least three hundred words by my estimation. I know he understands *go* and *danger*. I know he can follow short, simple sentences. Finally, his face clouds over and a low whimper escapes his lips.

"It will be all right," I say. "You'll have fun here. We'll try to come back, I promise. We'll miss you so much."

I run my fingers through the black fur on his back. I scratch behind his ears, his favorite spot, and press a kiss to his soft muzzle. I will miss him with every fiber of my being, but maybe Finn's right, maybe this separation is for the best. Maybe it's better for him not to be tethered to us and our dangerous lives. We are wanted and we'll be hunted forever, but he is free to roam this forest.

Shy Boy hides his face in his hands when Zoe, Tilly, Nya and Scout emerge from the trees. They've been intrigued by Shy Boy for so long, and this might be their last chance to interact with him, to witness his gentle soul.

Shy Boy trusts Pip and me completely and he's even warmed up to Finn, but he is reluctant to open up to such a large group of humans.

"Silly thing," Zoe says gently. "Closing your eyes won't make us disappear."

Shy Boy peeks at her through an opening between his fingers.

"It's okay, Shy Boy," Pip reassures him. "Those are our friends. They want to say goodbye, too."

"Can I touch him?" Tilly asks.

I gently take Shy Boy's hand and offer it to her, bridging the gap between them.

He doesn't pull away, which surprises me at first, but when I let go of his hand, he immediately panics. He calms only when I pull him close, when he feels the familiar comfort of my embrace. Maybe we would have both been better off if we hadn't met at all. My eyes well up as I realize it's time to let go.

I pat his head one last time while the girls each take a turn hugging him.

Then it's Pip's turn. Her eyes brim with tears. "Goodbye, Shy Boy. I will never forget you. I'll come back for you with Freya and Finn, and we'll be a family again."

"Goodbye, Shy Boy," I whisper. "You will always be in my heart."

◈

WE WALK BACK TO the camp with our heads hung low and our hearts sunk, feeling deep within the finality of what lies ahead. Pip and I have bonded with Shy Boy, but all of us have sensed his disappointment and quiet sadness. We're leaving a whole bright world behind us to hide in a dark, claustrophobic dungeon.

Finn and Theo approach us. Tilly, our newly appointed matchmaker, nudges Nya, then pinches her arm. Nya yelps and her crutch clatters to the ground. Zoe gets it for her, shooting Tilly a warning glare.

"Are you guys doing okay?" Finn asks as he hurries to help Nya.

"Sure, we're fine. Just saying goodbye. Where are you two headed?" Zoe says.

"Looking for you," Theo says. "We thought you might want to hit the training ring before we pack up everything."

"Okay, yes, we're in," Zoe says.

Our final day of training in this mountain camp. It's anyone's guess when it will be safe for us to come back and live out in the open again. If it will ever be safe once the drones start patrolling the skies, watching every move on the ground. The weight of my responsibility suddenly feels a thousand times heavier.

"We said goodbye to Shy Boy," I tell Finn. I want to dive into his arms and let my tears spill, but we are not alone.

"You have him in your heart, and he has you in his," Finn says. "You can carry each other wherever you go. Love transcends physical space, Freya."

"I wish I had your faith in things."

"All you have to do is decide to have it. It's a choice. You just have to let go of your fears."

"Is life really so easy for you, Finn?" Sometimes he eludes me, almost as if he's living on a different plane of reality.

"What are you two talking about?" Tilly says, interrupting us.

"Shy Boy," I say, but then I realize that her question was merely a pretext. Her eyes are fixed on Nya and Theo who are walking ahead of us. Theo's arm is wrapped around her waist to support her. Nya doesn't waste time once she's made up her mind.

"What are we looking at?" Finn says, following my gaze.

"Nothing," I say with mixed feelings. Is he blind to the concept of love, or is he just blind to seeing me as a woman?

His expression changes to dead serious. "We need to talk," he says. "Alone."

CHAPTER 8

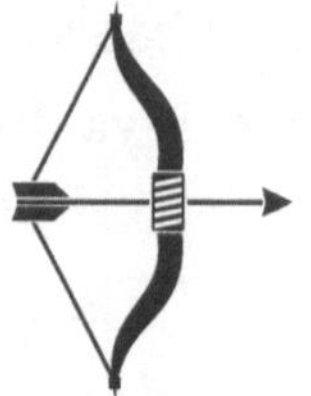

I'VE BECOME A MASTER of avoidance and artful evasion. I managed to postpone, dodge, and deflect all of Finn's attempts to corner me for a conversation. He tried several times last night and then again this morning, but I made myself unavailable, what with the training, the frantic packing for our trip, and the excuse of spending time with Pip. Pathetic really. I'm more consumed by my own anxieties about my future with Finn than I am with the impending doom facing our entire planet, it seems.

The Sliman returned late in the afternoon. They explained that the plantations are in chaos, reeling from the aftermath of our attack on the convoy. The response is what we expected: the first drones will arrive in three days' time and change the playing field forever.

Wudak insisted that if not for the Sliman rebels' help and their willingness to risk everything, we would be crushed the moment those drones darkened our skies.

We set out in the early evening. The Sliman brought a stretcher for Nya, but she stubbornly prefers to hobble along on her own two feet for most of the way. No matter the circumstances, Nya will never give in. She is, and always will be, a warrior.

The Sliman told us it will take us several hours to reach their subterranean base. We don't mind walking long distances, but between the weight of the supplies we have to carry and the onslaught of memories the forest brings rushing back, the journey seems to take an eternity.

We skirt the edge of the forest that surrounds our abandoned facilities, the place where we spent two years honing our skills, forging our bonds and preparing for war. The place where I struggled to prove my worth and earn my place in the team—also the place where Daphne was alive, vibrant and thriving.

Thinking about Daphne as we stroll through the dark forest hurts as much as it did the night we lost her. Her beauty, her strength, her courage, the way she sacrificed herself to save Damian and me... these are things that I can never forget.

I believe we are connected now, Daphne and I. She reached out to me in her final hour and mended our strenuous relationship with her one last gesture of self-giving. There's nothing I wouldn't give to bring her back. I would have gladly traded places with her. But Daphne was prepared to die that day; she willingly walked into the line of fire and sealed her own fate.

Damian and I have been unable to speak about Daphne since the night she died, but I know with a bone-deep certainty that we *need* to talk about her. Everything we do, everything we say to each other is overwrought by her memory. She's become an invisible wall between us, a constant reminder of what we have lost.

I have a feeling that he senses it, too—that persistent, unspoken presence. He tries too hard to project his mixed emotions, to force them onto what I represent to him now. He misses Daphne more than he ever thought possible. Her love for him has grown in value now that it's gone. He needs closure, absolution, or maybe he just needs something to fill the void, and he's convinced himself that I can do that.

I shake my head to clear my thoughts. Wudak is doing his best to stay close to me like a watchful guardian and I'm doing my best to escape him, yet he always ends up beside me, behind me or right in my path. I understand that he wouldn't be here, risking his life, if it weren't for me and my unique mutation, but that knowledge doesn't make me feel any less uncomfortable.

We leave the forest behind and head south through rolling hills. We're lucky to have a clear sky tonight, but then Wudak abruptly orders us to halt in the middle of nowhere. We're surrounded by gnarled shrubs and thorny hedge plants. In the far distance, barely visible in the moonlight, we can just make out the jagged peaks of the southern sierras.

Gritu turns his handheld sensor to the east. The device emits a high-pitched beeping sound instantly. He walks eastward and the beeping gets louder and more insistent. Then all of a sudden, it stops.

"It's here," Gritu says and kicks the ground with the heel of his boot. Malzod and Wudak go to him and all three drop to their knees, their hands probing the earth.

I turn to Finn, puzzled. He shrugs and turns his attention back to whatever ritual the three Sliman are performing.

Moments later, the Sliman pry open some sort of hidden trapdoor, revealing a gaping hole. They urge us to climb down as fast as possible.

"Just jump," Wudak says as he senses my hesitation. All I can see is a bottomless black hole. "Trust starts here, Freya." His words resonate deep within. I take a deep breath and jump down the hole, surrendering myself to the darkness.

I land safely in what appears to be the beginning of a long tunnel. In the distance, I can just make out the light of a single big torch mounted on the wall. Instinctively, I reach out and grab Finn's hand who's just landed behind me.

Once everyone has landed, we begin to stagger down

the long tunnel as it goes deeper and deeper. Wudak moves ahead and unhooks the torch that casts long, dancing shadows that distort the tunnel walls as he advances. We follow the Sliman in absolute silence.

We walk for ten or fifteen minutes, or perhaps much longer, before we reach a crossroads, an intersection of tunnels carved into the earth. The tunnel we've been following continues straight ahead, but another tunnel crosses it, offering an impossible choice: we could go either left or right. The sheer vastness of this subterranean labyrinth is overwhelming.

Wudak motions to us to continue straight ahead. I catch a glimpse of some carvings on the tunnel walls. I stop for a moment to take a closer look, but Wudak insists that we have to keep moving. There's no time for idle curiosity.

The tunnel opens up to a big, round cavern, lit by a scattering of torches and candles on a small wooden table. Wax is dripping down the ornate silver candleholders and the flames are trembling. There must be a ventilation system in the tunnels, but I can't locate it.

Wudak leads us to a small opening in the back of the cavern. "This is where our lodgings begin," he says. His voice echoes in the cavern. "Many of our allies have braved the journey here to welcome you."

I expect Wudak to usher us through the opening, but instead he retraces his steps to the tunnel at the opposite end of the cavern. He searches the rough stone wall meticulously where the tunnel meets the cavern. He finds what he's looking for, a barely perceptible seam in the rock, and presses against it.

The result is both immediate and startling. A section of the wall, roughly six feet high and two feet wide, caves inward with a groan, giving way to a hidden tunnel.

We walk inside the newly revealed passage for several minutes as it winds and twists before it widens into another rounded cavern with smooth walls, almost identical to the last one but much bigger. In the center, there's a long table made of rough-hewn wood with red metallic chairs that look completely out of place. Twenty Sliman with impassive faces stand rigidly against the walls around the cave, menacingly imposing in their black uniforms that seem to blend with the shadows.

As if controlled by a silent command, all eyes turn to me, intense and curious. They have recognized me, *the alien bride*, the potential key to their survival. I realize with a jolt of embarrassment, that I'm clutching Finn's hand. I release it immediately, my cheeks burning.

The Sliman bow their heads as a sign of recognition, crossing their arms on their chests. *The infamous Sliman salute.* Ugly memories flood back: the cold, sterile environment of the plantations, the rigid discipline, the constant surveillance. We will all have to adjust to this new reality of having Sliman allies.

I steal a glance at Damian for the first time all day. He's doing his best to maintain control and not order us to get the hell out of this hellhole, but the tension radiates from him, a barely contained fury threatening to erupt. All of us, I realize, look stunned and uncertain. We are not in control here. We are pawns in a much larger game.

"We'll take you to your quarters now," Wudak says. "You can settle in and get some rest. We'll meet again in the morning and make the necessary introductions."

One of the Sliman we've just met reaches under the table to pull a hidden lever, and a door opens.

"Who designed this place?" Theo whispers.

"Zolkon," Wudak says, offering no further explanation, no context, no hint of who or what Zolkon might be.

We are herded through the door and down an endless hallway lined with identical wooden doors on both sides. Each door is marked with a number, sequentially ordered. We pass numbers 1, 2, 3... 10... 20, the numbers climbing higher with each step until the Sliman halt before door number 40.

"Numbers 41 through 52 are yours," Wudak says. "Each of you can have a private room. Choose whichever you prefer, though they are, in all respects, identical. You will find water, food, and a selection of clothing inside, should you wish to change. We trust you will find something that fits."

I'm speechless. Our hosts have anticipated almost every need. The level of preparation hints at a level of control that is deeply unsettling.

"Door No 55 is a library," Gritu says. "You are fond of books, are you not?"

Well, I stand corrected. Not *almost* every need. They have seemingly anticipated everything. Do they know about Lost Town and the library we risked our lives to access? Have they been subtly manipulating our actions all along? Have they been covering up for us this entire time while we were stupid enough to think our actions went unnoticed?

One of the Sliman introduces himself as Quax before producing a chain of keys from his pocket. He starts to unlock the doors one by one, pushing them wide open.

The rooms are neat and tidy. Each contains a comfortable bed, a desk and a chair, a closet and a sink. Torches are mounted on the walls, and a single candle sits on every desk.

"Is there no electricity in the base?" I ask Wudak.

"There is, but we prefer to conserve it for essential things," he says. "I will show you some of those uses tomorrow. I can, of course, arrange to have electricity in your room if you so wish."

I try to force a smile. "No, that's perfectly fine. I was just wondering out loud."

"I must take my leave," Wudak says, his gaze lingering

on me for a moment. "Quax will attend to your needs. Do not hesitate to ask him for anything you require."

I nod and he's gone along with Gritu, Malzod and three more Sliman that escorted us here. Only Quax remains, standing rigidly at attention. He is the epitome of the Sliman kind: tall, strong, efficient, obedient, impassive, unwavering, but his frame is heavier than most. On his left cheek, there's a tattoo of a yellow rose.

All the doors to our rooms are open now, but Quax stays put. "At your service," he says to me, clicking his polished boots together.

"That's... that's all, I think," I say, striving for a casual tone. After a moment of awkward silence, I add, "Thank you, Quax."

"My pleasure," he says but still makes no move to leave.

"Um, you can go now." I can't be any clearer than that, can I?

"We're all like tomatoes," he says, his expression unchanged.

"Tomatoes?" Biscuit inquires, interested now.

"Yes, one gene taken out, one gene injected in. Perfect outcome. We're all the same. Mutants."

By *we*, he means the Sliman and the Saviors. We realize that when he smiles, revealing a set of gray teeth.

"We'll take it from here, Quax, thank you," I say as I practically shove him down the hallway.

"Should we draw to decide who gets which room?" Zoe

says when Quax is gone.

Damian, who has been silent and brooding since we entered the tunnels, decides to speak finally. "Who cares?" he says, irritated. "Just pick a damn door and lock yourself inside."

This entire experience must be far more difficult for him than it is on anyone else. He must feel like he has relinquished all control, surrendering his authority to the Sliman, and for some reason it bothers me that he should feel that way. I know how much he values his position and his ability to protect us, but there's nothing I can do to change the situation.

I turn to my sister. "Okay, Pip, we can share a room."

Pip shakes her head. "No, no, Freya. I never had a room of my own before." She pauses to think for a moment. "I want... I want door number 45."

Her decisiveness is refreshing. We could all use some of that right now.

I reach out and squeeze her hand. "Then I guess I'll take 47, so we're right next to each other."

Finn is quick to act as always. He chooses door number 46, directly across the hall from Pip and me. Damian, predictably, walks down the hallway to the very last door. He's always preferred his own company, but something on his face tells me that this time he'd have preferred to stay right in the middle of the group if only it hadn't been for the fact that he'd then have to be close to *me*.

I don't know... maybe it's all in my head. Maybe I'm projecting my insecurities onto him. No matter what his flaws are, no matter how gruff he can be, Damian's not one to let emotions get the better of him. He'd fight for each and every one of us no matter what.

When I enter my room, I plop down on the bed, feeling completely drained. I could just lie down, close my eyes and drift off to dreamland. It could easily go the wrong way, of course, and I could end up in nightmare-land instead.

I take off my boots, prop my feet up on a cushion and lean back against the soft headboard. I've never seen a bed like this before, let alone sleep in one. The candle on the desk smells of vanilla and cinnamon, probably an attempt at creating a sense of comfort and home. I want to take everything in, to catalog every detail before I doze off. I get up and sit at the desk. I find a pen and a notebook in the desk drawer and write down my name on the first page, followed by a silly sentence: *Freya has been here.*

I take off my jacket and carefully hang it on the back of the chair. Behind a worn flask and a couple of mismatched dishes, I spot a small mirror. I hold it up to my face, taking a long, critical look at my reflection. My lips are chapped and dark circles have formed under my eyes. My hair is a wild, frizzy mess, tangled with twigs, leaves and other unidentifiable things. I look ragged, worn and in need of rest.

With a sigh, I pull out my brush and eye the clean shirt and pants folded neatly at the foot of the bed. Maybe some fresh clothes will help me feel human again.

A soft knock on the door shatters the perfect silence.

"Who is it?" I ask, startled.

"It's Finn."

I crack the door open, just enough to stick my neck out. "Is everything okay?"

"Yeah, I guess so. This place is terribly quiet. It's driving me nuts."

I know exactly what he means. In the forest, silence is an illusion. Life is a constant hum, a symphony of rustling leaves, chirping insects and cooing birds. Even in the dead of night, the forest never truly sleeps.

"Won't you let me in?" Finn says, gently pushing against the door to open it wider. I push back with equal force. "We need to talk, remember?" he insists.

So, he hasn't forgotten. Whatever it is that he wants to tell me is clearly of great importance to him.

"Not now, Finn. I'm beat. I can't even think straight."

He doesn't even try to hide the disappointment in his voice. "Tomorrow then," he says, resigned, then turns and walks back to his room across the hall.

Nerves twist in my gut and my mind kicks into overdrive. Any hope of sleep flies out the window. I have no idea how much longer I'll be able to put him off, or even why I'd want to.

CHAPTER 9

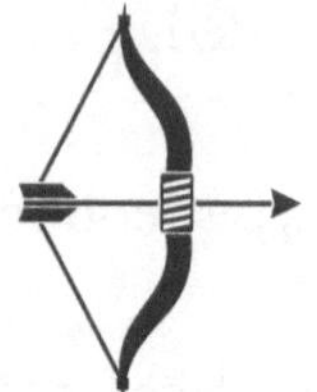

WUDAK AND I STEP out of the cavern where we snacked and walk down the long, echoing hallway to reach a big iron gate at the end. Wudak unlocks it, pushes it open and leads the way into a pitch-black area. When he lights the torches that hang from hooks along the walls, the sheer vastness of the chamber leaves me breathless.

Two long tables run parallel along the walls, covered with an arsenal of weapons—pulse guns, magnetic blades, shock bows, and alien instruments of war I've never seen before. There are two simulation pods in the back and a fenced-in combat ring right in the center.

A training cavern. No, more than that—a place to prepare for battle and become warriors.

"We designed it for you," Wudak says. "We can change it to fit your needs. Just tell me what you want and we'll do it."

This is no joke. Wudak and his rebel Sliman will do as I say. I realize that now. Wudak has repeated it on a number of occasions, but this is the first time I actually come to believe it. I have an army of my own. A dark army for a brighter future.

I let my fingers run over the array of guns and weapons on the tables. My hands feel impatient. I want to get in the simulators. I want to target practice. I want to fight.

Wudak reads my mind. "You should concentrate on the receptor," he says. "There's nothing more powerful or more demanding on the planet. It could destroy everything, including you. You have to learn to control it."

"I'm ready. I will do as you say."

"I am pleased," he says. I swear I see something that resembles a smile on his face. I instinctively reach out to pat him on the shoulder, but he recoils as if a snake had just climbed on him.

"I'm sorry," I say, wishing I'd be less impulsive sometimes.

"It is I who am sorry," Wudak says. "Nobody has ever touched me before. Not unless they intended to harm me."

I nod and take the sensory receptor out of my pocket.

Wudak narrows his eyes. "Such a small thing," he says, "yet so devastating."

"It can also be used for good," I say. "I know it. I've seen it. It made Daphne's passing peaceful."

Wudak's glance is questioning but also respectful.

"Daphne was my friend," I say. "She died during the fight against the aliens."

"The receptor's energy can be used to heal physical and emotional wounds," he says. "It can also produce energy to be converted into electricity and fuel. But there's no time to teach you all that. You will probably figure it out on your own over time. Now you must learn to fight. And win."

He bows and I do the same. I don't know why, but it seems like the appropriate thing to do. Wudak walks to the other side of the room.

"Just know that I will protect you with my life," he says and, within a split second, he charges at me with a magnetic knife in his hand.

I barely have time to think. Those knives never miss their target. They are drawn to bones and cartilage like moths to a flame. Once they enter your body, they fuse with the bones and cannot be retrieved. Only a skilled surgeon can remove them without destroying the surrounding bones, nerves and tissues completely.

I have a couple of seconds to process all this and react. The receptor starts flashing and Wudak is lifted off the ground and thrown against the wall.

"Good," he says as he hoists himself up. "You have some skill already."

"What did you think? That you'd have to train a help-less little girl?" I say, feeling my adrenaline rising at the prospect of more sparring with Wudak.

"I didn't think anything," he says. "But you are right. You are a little girl."

He's right in the strict sense of the word. I'm small, but I've been training and fighting all my life, and I'm a lot stronger than I look. And I'll be turning nineteen soon. I won't be a girl for long.

In a moment, Wudak swerves his body and hits me on the stomach with his elbow, knocking the wind out of me. I try to say something, but I find myself unable to speak. I fall to my knees.

"You have to stay focused," he says. "That is your biggest weakness. You get too pleased too soon. My guess is you get too sad too soon also. Like right now?"

"Get lost, Wudak," I manage to say as I struggle to get back up on my feet.

"You're becoming angry. Now we might be getting somewhere," he says. "Never be pleased with yourself. That's my first lesson to you. Complacency will kill you as surely as a magnetic knife."

"Your lessons carry bruises," I say. "At least you mean well." Before I'm even done speaking, I find my back against the wall with Wudak's forearm pressing my throat.

"Lesson number two. Never trust a Sliman," he says

as he gradually releases the pressure on my throat. "Not unless they're under my command," he adds sarcastically.

I rub my throat with my left hand. My right hand starts to itch with the desire to use the receptor against him. I don't want to hurt him, but he seems to have no problem hurting me. Maybe that's another lesson he's trying to impress on me. There's no room for sensitivities.

"The sensory receptor must become a part of you," he says as he picks up a pulse gun. "It's not good enough that you know how to use it in an emergency or when you get angry or scared. It's not good enough that you know how to connect to it or how to send your brainwave messages down your arm. It's not good enough that you know about all the things you can do with it, whether it is to attack or to defend."

"What is good enough then?" I say, exasperated.

"You become it, and it becomes you. It responds to your dreams when you sleep. It does what you order it to do even when you have no physical contact with it. It becomes second nature, like walking or running. That's what's good enough."

I smile. "You must be out of your mind."

"Give it to me," he says, extending his hand.

"No," I say firmly.

"Freya, give me the receptor."

I close my eyes for a heartbeat, and when I open them again, I've made my choice. I hand over the receptor, placing my trust in him. It's not like he can use it anyway.

But the moment he takes it from me, he presses the gun he's holding hard against my temple. "What are you going to do now?" he says, his voice smooth, almost mocking.

"I think I've had enough of your tricks for one day," I say, but I know that this will have no effect on him. He's got a mission, and I might as well accept it. I know what he wants from me.

I block out everything—fear, pain, doubt—and concentrate on one single point: the sensory receptor in Wudak's hand. The cold barrel of the pulse gun digs harder into my temple, sending a throbbing ache through my skull. My ears start ringing and my eyes burn, but I won't give in.

I shut out every sound, every sight, every thought but one—*power*. I repeat it silently, fiercely, again and again, until that single word fills my mind—until it becomes my truth. Then an electric jolt rockets up my spine and I know I've made the connection.

Wudak jerks and drops the receptor. A raw, deep red mark blooms across the palm of his hand. A burn mark.

"That's the spirit," he says as he spits on his palm. "Now try and pick the receptor up without touching it."

The very idea of going through this mental hell again puts me off completely. I don't have enough strength left in me.

I take Wudak's hand to look at the wound, but he pulls

away immediately. I have to remember that he doesn't like to be touched.

"This will need some cleaning and bandaging," I say.

"I will have it taken care of, no need for you to worry," he says coldly.

"I think I'm done for the time being. I didn't sleep very well and I don't feel like myself. Too much happening at the same time."

"I understand, but you cannot forget. Time is running out."

He walks me back to the hallway. Even from down here, I can see Finn sitting on the floor outside my room. So can Wudak.

"Your friend is impulsive and has a lot to learn, but his heart is in the right place," Wudak whispers.

"You talk as if you know everything about the human soul," I scold him, "even though you yourself admitted to not understanding us all that well."

"I might not understand the complexity of your emotions, but I do see through your intentions and reasoning," he says as he walks away.

I pause in front of Finn. He looks up from his touchpad and greets me with a smile. I can't turn him away, not this time. And even though I feel more tired than ever, using my fatigue as an excuse again will only make him suspicious.

I open my door and invite him in. "Where's everyone?"

"Visiting what the Sliman call the Labs."

"The Labs? Where's that?"

"There's a gate between doors 14 and 16. Barely noticeable if you don't know it's there," he says as he sits down on the bed.

"Why didn't you go?" I ask, but I know the answer.

"You know I've been wanting to talk to you, Tick."

There we go. I can't pinpoint exactly what scares me about what he's going to tell me. This is Finn after all. We can talk about everything. What I do know is that I feel terribly guilty.

He invites me to sit down next to him. "How are you holding up?" he says.

I shrug. "It's all so bizarre, isn't it? So much has changed during the past few months. Wudak just showed me that I can use the receptor without touching it."

The information I offer amazes him. "You can really do that?" he says with a new spark in his eyes.

"Yes... well, I'm a long way from being in control of the process, but it can be done, yes."

"That's good, Tick," he says and takes my hand in his. "We can all use some good news."

I notice the strain in his voice, the effort it takes for him to smile. Why haven't I noticed this already? I should be begging him to share his thoughts with me, not hiding from him.

"Finn, what's wrong? Tell me," I manage to say.

"It's that obvious, huh? Listen, Tick, I've been thinking a lot. About Daphne, about my promise to her. Remember that box I hid for her? I think I have to go get it and bring it to Damian like she wanted me to."

This is not what I expected to hear. Not even close. "It's dangerous, Finn. You know that. You can't get that close to our old facilities. The place must be swarming with guards and sensors."

"I have to give it a try, Tick. I don't think I'll be able to live with myself otherwise."

"It's too soon, Finn. You have to give it some time."

"I have. It's been almost three months and Damian still doesn't know."

My hands fly to his shoulders, gripping them tight. "Tell him then. You'll see that he won't let you go."

"I know that he won't, and not just because he's worried about my safety. Which is why I won't tell him."

"Why do you have to be so stubborn?" I shove him back, frustrated. Then I think about what he has just said. "Wait, what do you mean he's not just worried about your safety? What else?"

"The box itself," he says.

"Why would he be worried about the box? He doesn't even know it exists."

"It doesn't matter, Freya. What matters is that I have to get it because I promised I would."

I almost push him again, but I won't be able to knock

any sense into him. He has been working this out for a long time. He's not going to give up. Not with the box being only a couple of hours away.

I have to do something fast. I throw my arms around his neck. "Finn, I can't lose you. Not like that. Not over something that can wait."

I move in and kiss his lips. He's too astonished to react at first. Then he runs his fingers through my messy hair and kisses me back. His kiss is gentle, patient, trusting. It strikes me that there's no passion to it, but it feels good to be so close to him. I feel that this is where I should be. We belong together and he deserves all my loyalty for the rest of my life. Finn makes sense in this crazy world. I love him in a way that I will never love another human being, but this is also why such a cataclysmic shift in our friendship scares me.

Finn has been my sounding board for so long that the idea of us falling out over a failed romance terrifies me. Relationships fall apart; longtime friends get bored with each other once they become lovers. The old books and movies show that happening all the time.

So, there's that. And then there's Damian. I can't shake the idea that I have failed him repeatedly ever since he saved my life. How can I disregard him completely?

"Where's your mind off to?" Finn asks, holding my face in his hands.

"I'm not doing this to make you do what I want," I say.

"I know."

"I still don't want you to go."

"I won't."

"Thank you," I say, relieved. "Finn, I don't know what I'm doing."

"Silly Tick, it's okay, you never know what you're doing anyway. We'll figure it out together."

I start crying and I can't stop myself. He's too good, too patient, too forgiving. My whole body shakes violently. I have nothing left in me. I have never cried like this, and I don't know how to stop it, how to conquer this despair.

Finn does what he always does—he holds me, comforts me. "Freya, I won't go, I promise you. Stop crying, okay? You're scaring me."

"It's okay," I say. "This is good. I wish I would have done it long ago."

"You did. A long, long time ago. When you were a baby."

"Are you calling me a baby?" I say, remembering Finn can also be a jerk.

"If it talks like one and cries like one..."

Words are no longer enough, so I pinch his arm.

"Now you've done it," he says, and I know that can only mean one thing.

"Stay away from me, you stupid boy," I say, but I'm already laughing, anticipating the tickling.

Finn laughs, too. "I'm not going to do this to you," he says. "Relax."

"Just psychological terror, huh?"

He doesn't answer. We hear steps down the hallway approaching fast.

"They're back," Finn says. "Let's go see what they have to say about the Labs."

He springs up to his feet. Every fiber in me wants to stop him from opening that door and letting everyone know he's been in my room. I'm a despicable person. I have manipulated his trust to control him, to prevent him from doing something I don't want him to do.

I follow Finn to the hallway. There's a lot of chattering going on, but I can't make out anything. The only thing I take in is the way Damian averts his glance from me a second after I enter the hall with Finn.

CHAPTER 10

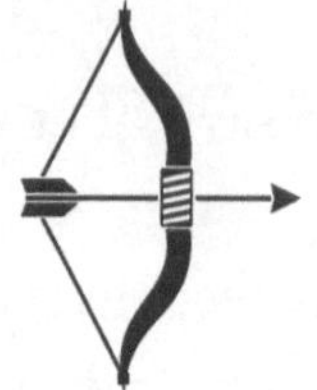

I WAKE UP TO the sensation of distant screaming in my ears. I try to open my eyelids, but the instant jolt of pain forces me to keep them shut. I sit up, rubbing my eyes before attempting to open them again. It's pitch black in the room. I reach for the candle and matches on the desk, but my fingers find empty space. Then I remember the receptor. In an instant, the room is illuminated. To my horror, I realize the screaming is real. It's coming through the walls from the next room.

Pip.

I snatch the receptor and bolt for the hallway, nearly bumping into Finn who's already outside Pip's room. By the time we open the door, most of the Saviors are gathered in the hallway.

Finn and I rush inside. Pip is on the floor, shaking. She looks ghostly pale and has tears in her eyes. Finn scoops her up and puts her back on the bed. I rush to her side and wrap my arms around her.

"What's wrong, Pip?"

"They're coming. They'll take me again," she sobs.

"It was a dream, Pip. You're safe," Finn says, trying to comfort her.

She shakes her head. "No, it's not a dream. They are coming. The dark army is coming. The scary ones will make them come."

I touch her forehead. It's burning hot. "Get Doc," I tell Finn. He disappears and a moment later, he returns with Doc.

Doc examines Pip while Finn and I step outside. My pulse is thrumming with unease.

The dark army is coming.

"Is Pip okay?" Zoe asks.

"I think she was having nightmares. About the plantation," I say.

"Is it possible she's starting to remember things?" Damian asks, arching his eyebrows.

"It's possible, I guess."

I need to talk to Wudak about this. If what he did to Pip with the hypnosis triggered this nightmare, then he should fix it. He claims he wants to serve me after all—now's his chance to prove it. But maybe Damian's right. Maybe this isn't a side effect but the desired outcome—maybe Pip's memories are starting to resurface.

Wudak said he'd help Pip through them. Either way, I need answers and Wudak is the only one who might give them to me.

"I'll go talk to Wudak," I say.

Damian grabs my arm before I can take a single step. "You're going to do what?"

"I'll go talk to Wudak about Pip."

"You'll actually go around the tunnels in the middle of the night trying to find a Sliman? You don't even know if he's here."

"I know it sounds crazy, but the receptor will guide me to him. I know it will."

"You will stay right here." There's nothing pleasant about the tone of his voice.

I jerk my arm off his grip. "Pip is my priority. I'll do whatever it takes."

"You cannot befriend Wudak," Damian snaps at me. His face goes red, his veins pulsing in his temples. He yells at me now. He's full-blown vintage Damian, only worse. "Are you out of your mind? Wudak is not your ally. He is not your friend. Everything he does, he does with an ulterior motive and wants something in return. Let him teach you how to use the damned receptor, but that's all."

The tunnels reverberate with his voice. He's never been so loud with me before. Even back when butting heads with him was on the daily menu, he always showed a certain restraint.

I feel like an idiot and I can't come up with anything to say.

Doc comes out of Pip's room. "Keep it low. I just managed to get her to sleep. I think she had a panic attack brought on by a nightmare."

"Thank you, Doc," I say with quivering lips.

I step inside the room. Pip looks peaceful and calm in her sleep. I kiss her forehead and wish her goodnight. Finn waits for me at the door.

"I should have said something to Damian," he says. "He was way off base yelling at you like that. In this place. With Sliman all around. It doesn't make sense."

"It's okay, I can handle Damian. You don't need to run interference for me anymore. He caught me off guard but next time he won't be so lucky."

Finn hesitates for a moment. "Freya, you'll probably want to kill me for this, but I agree with Damian. Don't think you can be friends with Wudak or any other Sliman. We don't know what their endgame is."

He's wrong, I don't want to kill him. I feel empty and lonely, and I want to stay up all night talking to him. We did that a lot at the breeding village. Even in Plantation-8 we stayed up a couple of times, risking our lives. In the camp we talked endlessly during our midnight watches together. We talked in the forest, gazing at the stars. We have talked about anything imaginable, and I miss that sort of interaction. There never seems to be time for things like that anymore. Every time we are together, it feels like we're stealing time.

"Try and get some rest," he says. "You look terrible."

"You really know how to flatter," I say, but I can already feel my eyelids getting heavy. I haven't slept properly in days.

I watch Finn as he walks to his room and then I shut my door. I drop myself onto the bed, lying on my stomach. Then the door opens and Damian waltzes in.

I sit up, throwing him an indignant glance. "I have nothing to say to you."

"Good, cause all you have to do is listen."

I immediately feel the urge to smack him across the face. "You don't ever yell at me like that again, do you hear me?" I hurl at him.

"I know you think I'm being unreasonable, unfair, maybe even insane, but I cannot stress this enough. Do not get cozy with Wudak. Nothing good will come out of it."

"You're overreacting. I know who Wudak is, what he wants. I'm not an idiot. I also know that for the moment he will do as I say." I talk in the calmest voice I can muster, but a wave of rage builds up slowly inside me to a degree I have never felt before. His outburst has damaged something between us. Something that I can't name, but I know it won't be repaired that easily. He probably knows it, too. That's why he's here.

"I wonder, do you believe the things you say? Don't you realize he's trying to gain your trust? It's a plan, Freya. He knows I see right through him, that's why he *warned* you about me."

"So why did you bring us here then?"

"Because there is no other choice. I'm not saying he's lying about the alien drones. He's lying as to why he wants to protect us from them. The sooner we're out of here, the better."

"You can't have second thoughts about this, you know that, Damian. Second thoughts lead to poor judgment, those are your words."

"I'm not having second thoughts, it is what it is. I just need you to be on the same page."

What he says makes sense. I know I'm not above reproach. I have been too quick to judge in the past, I have said the wrong things again and again.

"Of course we're on the same page," I say. "I trust you, Damian. I know you'll do the right thing. Why can't you trust me, too?"

He takes a couple of steps and kneels in front of me.

"Don't do this," I say and make a move to get up.

"Please, sit down," he says. "Hear me out."

I decide to humor him. "You have five minutes. I'm exhausted and I might fall asleep any moment."

"Good enough. I'm worried about you, Freya," he says. "You react without thinking. You're on the defense a lot more than you're on the offense."

"That's only true when it comes to you," I blurt out and almost immediately realize the immensity of the mistake I have made.

He locks his eyes with mine while he thinks about this. "And why is that?"

"Let me see, because you are insufferable and infuriating?" I try to joke, but I know he can't be fooled that easily.

"You know what I think? I think you're having a really hard time trying to come to terms with your feelings for me."

Yep, there it is, we're back to square one. "Please, you're so full of yourself."

"Running to Finn every time you want to stop thinking about me isn't going to fix this."

"Get out, Damian. Your five minutes are up."

His expression changes from somber to downright mocking. "That's your response to pretty much everything I do or say."

"You promised you'd stop bothering me with all this," I remind him.

"I would if I thought that's what you really wanted."

"We can't have a relationship; I don't know how many times I've told you already. Besides, why would you even want to? You've done nothing but despise me for most of the time we've known each other."

"People can change their mind," he says, shrugging.

"Okay, do you want to know what *I* think? I think you started projecting your feelings for Daphne on me the night she died. I'm sorry but it had to be said."

I have touched a nerve. "Freya, do not repeat that ever again."

"It's true though, isn't it? Guilt has overwhelmed you. It has changed you. We both know we wouldn't even be standing here if it weren't for her. But we can't chase that pain away by pretending we mean something to each other all of a sudden. We can't make this right, Damian."

This finally gets to him. He stands up. "It's pointless. Nobody can get through to you. Just stay away from Wudak beyond the training hours."

He leaves and the room starts spinning. I lie back on the pillows, but I know I won't be able to sleep. I have to do something to put my mind at ease. I get up, cross the hallway and knock gently on Finn's door. I don't wait for an answer, I never do.

He's fast asleep. I can hear his strong, slow breathing in the dark.

"Finn," I whisper in his ear, "it's me, wake up. I need to tell you something."

He doesn't respond so I shove him softly. "Come on, open your eyes."

"Freya?" he whispers my name.

I turn on the receptor and a soft blue light fills the room.

Finn rubs his eyes. "What's wrong? Is it Pip?"

"No. Remember what you said about the box?"

He nods although he seems a bit disoriented still.

"You were right, we have to go get it, Finn."

"We?"

"You didn't really think I'd let you go by yourself, did you?"

Finn sits up and I see the muscles on his neck tensing. "You couldn't wait to tell me in the morning?"

"No, because we're going tomorrow. It will be our last chance before the drones arrive."

"This is insane, Freya. I'll go when I feel like it and you are not going with me."

"The hell I'm not. You'll never make it out of there alive on your own. I have the receptor and I'm beginning to think there's nothing it won't do if I will it. We are going tomorrow night. We'll sneak out. We'll be back before anyone knows we're gone. Trust me, it's the best way."

I can see he's still not convinced. "Why the sudden change of heart?"

"The sooner we get that box back, the better. That way we can both stop thinking about it."

I leave his room quickly and return to mine. I feel satisfied that this plan might finally break Damian free of his weird fascination with me. I close my eyes and sleep invades me fast. It's easier to fall asleep when you have a plan.

CHAPTER 11

Finn crouches down to check the fresh prints on the wet leaves. The drizzle has stopped but everything's still damp and glistening with moisture.

"It's okay," he says. "They're animal tracks. Probably a lone wolf."

There are very few wolves left in the forest and they're too scared to venture into the open. They stay hidden in the shadows and only emerge at night in search of prey. The Sliman have made sure of that.

We have covered more than half the distance to where Finn hid the box. He's marked the tree with red ink, something I didn't notice the night I followed him. I think I could find the tree on my own anyway. The memory of that night is still very vivid and so I can retrace every single step I took with unsettling accuracy.

The sensory receptor hums in my hand as I project

a shield around us—a shimmering mist of light purple energy. Radars and sensors won't be able to penetrate it unless my focus slips completely. It doesn't take much effort to maintain the energy anyway, since there are only two of us inside the shield and we stay close together.

My brain can handle two tasks at the same time with growing ease. I can hold the shield steady while listening and responding to everything Finn says. A third factor would make the equation trickier, but for now, I can manage.

The night air is crisp and fresh. I've missed the sounds and smells of our forest, the familiarity of its unrest. Finn feels it, too. He walks just behind me, scanning the trees and bushes through the faint light the receptor casts around us.

Everything reminds us of our life here. Every leaf, every trunk, every nocturnal creature has a story to tell about the expectations and disappointments we experienced, the triumphs, the failures, the quiet moments of hope and devastation.

We're only a few hundred yards away from camp now. The images from our last night in the forest attack me with sharp clarity. In my mind, I see Finn walk cautiously out of the camp with the nimbleness of a feline. I see him come to a halt in front of a massive tree, kneel and press his hands into the earth. I see the small box in his palm before he buries it in the ground. I hear my fast heartbeat, feel the sweat on my face and hands.

Finn's voice pulls me back. "It's here."

I blink, my gaze locking onto the tree he's pointing at—a towering, ancient giant, exactly like the one in my vision.

He shows me the red mark on the tree, then presses his hand to the ground, searching for a soft spot. When he finds it, he glances at me.

"I need more light here," he says.

I concentrate, willing the receptor to glow brighter. We drop to our knees, scooping away the damp earth with our hands. The box emerges from the soil, smaller than I remember, barely the size of my palm, but when I hold it, it feels heavier than I thought it would be. Its weight presses into my skin like an unbearable burden.

"Do you have any idea what's in it?" I ask.

Finn shakes his head. "No, none whatsoever. Daphne was always secretive when it came to Damian."

"She did say that she loved him, right?"

"Yes. I told you that."

"Do you think he loved her back?"

Finn stands up, brushing dirt from his hands. "Not according to Daphne. We should head back, Freya. The sooner, the better."

"Could she have been wrong?" I insist.

"What difference would that make now, Freya?" he says impatiently.

"I don't know. It might explain why he's acting the way he does."

Finn exhales hard as he sits back down. "Would it explain why he kissed you the night Daphne died?" he says without looking at me.

His straightforwardness shocks me. It's the first time he's mentioned the kiss. This whole time I've felt like there's been a secret pact between us to never go there. I want to say something but can't figure out what that could be.

"You know I saw you," Finn goes on after a while.

"It was... it was a very strange moment," I manage to say. "I was caught off guard. I was in shock, Finn. So was Damian."

He shakes his head. "Freya, you know he came back for you that day. While I was putting your life at risk, while I hesitated, torn between fighting and running, while I was giving confusing orders and letting terrible things happen, he put his animosity for me aside." He locks his eyes on mine. "He came back and jumped in front of you. To protect you." His voice has a gravity I've never heard before.

"What are you talking about? He wasn't the only one who came back. Zoe, Theo, Doc... they didn't even know the kind of danger we were in. They changed their minds and came to find us, that's all. Then they acted instinctively."

Finn turns fully toward me now, his gaze sharp. "You didn't see his face when he thought you were going to get killed. I did."

I find it hard to breathe. I want him to stop talking.

"He cares about you, Freya, and you know it. So, the question now is, what are you going to do about it?"

"*Do* about it? Nothing. I don't plan on doing anything," I say stubbornly.

"You can't wish it away, Freya. It's there and it's staring at you. And I need to know the answer."

My head feels heavy. My focus is diminishing. I hold the receptor tighter and reinforce our shield.

"There's nothing to know, okay?"

"Why are you avoiding the question?"

"Stop it, Finn! Daphne is dead. Did you hear me? Dead. For him. He belongs to her. It's the only thing that makes sense. Everything else is just pointless."

"The only thing that makes sense is that he belongs to a ghost? It's the only thing that doesn't make sense, Freya. Why are we even here? What are you hoping to find?"

"This whole conversation is insane, Finn. Let's just go."

I push to my feet and walk away as fast as I can. I don't want to keep lying to him, but I can't betray Damian's trust either. I can't just tell Finn how Damian has been trying to get closer to me, or how I haven't been able to shut it down for good. And since I don't plan on letting anything happen between Damian and me, what's the point in even talking about it?

A sharp, whizzing sound shatters my thoughts. It's fast, slicing through the air like something mechanical and deadly.

"Freya!" Finn's voice is raw with anguish.

I spin around just in time to see him yanked upward, his body jerking as his left ankle snags in a loop. He dangles from a tree branch, swinging from side to side.

A wolf trap.

My stomach clenches. I have maybe five seconds before the concealed magnetic knives deploy automatically. I squeeze the receptor, channeling a focused beam of energy. The rope snaps and Finn drops, landing hard with a dull thud. A heartbeat later—*whip!* A magnetic knife hurtles through the air and hits the tree, burying itself in the hard flesh of the trunk, right where Finn's body would have been.

I hit the ground and crawl on my stomach to Finn. "Don't move," I cry out as he tries to lift his head.

I reach him as fast as I can. "Are you okay?" I ask, already using the receptor to scan his body for injuries.

"The shield," he whispers.

It's down. My focus has been divided. I flick it back on, but it might be too late. Our position could already be compromised.

"Let's get the hell out of here," I whisper. "You've got nothing broken."

We run. It's our only option. If we're lucky, the Sliman won't realize their trap failed and won't come looking for the prey that escaped. Maybe we can make it out of the forest and into the old escape tunnel before they track us.

Maybe.

"Do you have the box?" I ask Finn, gasping between breaths.

He nods, lifting his hand just enough for me to see the small shape clenched in his fist. We push forward, sprinting through the trees. I keep the shield in place, but I don't know how the bumpy motion of our wild escape is affecting it. I have no idea if it will hold.

We're nearing the edge of the forest. One more turn to the left and we'll enter the tunnel that will take us to the hills. If we make it there, we'll be able to reach the Sliman underground base in less than two hours. And if luck is on our side, we'll make it back before sunrise.

I glance at Finn, my pulse hammering, and force a smile, hoping for a truce, when a Sliman drops from a tree and blocks my way. I collide with him hard. I hear my bones crushing against his thickened skin. Sliman can do that—they can harden their bodies into impenetrable armor plates if they have enough time and concentration to prepare for the transformation.

A second Sliman attacks, but my main concern is the receptor. The collision has knocked it out of my grip. I scan the ground but can't find it. Wudak warned me about things like this, about how the receptor had to become a part of me if I were to summon its powers when provoked, scared or angry. When I was caught off guard.

The Sliman lunges, reaching for my arm, but I spin away, rolling back to my feet faster than he anticipates. My hand flies to my pulse gun, but so does his—and he's quicker than me. Within a split second, he has me at the end of his barrel, but he doesn't pull the trigger. He hesitates. Recognition flickers in his eerie green eyes. *I'm not supposed to be killed.*

It doesn't matter. His hesitation gives me enough time to fully comprehend the gravity of my predicament. I react instinctively. I call to the receptor. It explodes the Sliman into small pieces as it lands in my hand, unleashing a pulse of raw energy.

I whirl around. Finn has overpowered the second attacker, his boot pressed on the Sliman's throat. Finn knocks him unconscious with the butt of his pulse gun.

I run to him, but before I can reach him, heavy, pounding footsteps shake the ground. The forest trembles with the weight of an approaching army of Sliman.

"What now?" I ask Finn.

"We can take them on," he says. "I know we can."

"I don't know, Finn."

"I'll be right next to you. We can do it, Freya."

I nod. Finn grabs me and pushes me up the nearest tree. I scramble up, my fingers slipping against the damp bark as I haul myself higher. Finn follows immediately. He'd be at the top already if he didn't hold back to keep me steady.

Below us, the Sliman warriors march through the undergrowth. A moment later, they come to a standstill.

They've discovered the remains of their companions. Even if they hadn't, they would have felt our presence anyway. Sliman are hunters. Their sharpened senses cannot be fooled. Not when we're only a few feet away, when our scent lingers, and we've left marks and prints all over the place.

I count at least twenty of them. They sniff around the ground, looking in all directions, and then turn their eyes upward.

"Now," Finn whispers in my ear.

I unleash my fury on the Sliman. The sensory receptor attacks them with all the ferocity I can channel into it. A prolonged energy blast wipes away five Sliman before the rest scatter.

Finn jumps off to the next tree, then to the next and the next until he's out of my field of vision. The Sliman are hiding, and it won't be possible to blow them up with big energy explosions. We have to hunt them down one by one until they retreat. Finn knows that. He can move fast without making a single sound. They won't see him coming.

I scan the area below, but it's hard to make out details in the dark.

I wish Tilly was here with her bionic eyes and ears.

The receptor lights up with a buzz. It's a warning; it has sensed something. I look down. A dark figure is attempting to climb my tree. *Destroy him*, I think, and the receptor strikes the intruder with a booming lightning. I smell something burning and hear footsteps retreating in a hurry. Nobody wants to share the fate of the Sliman who got fried.

They know where I am now. They are no match for the receptor, but Wudak warned me there are ways around it. Especially when I can't see a single thing in the dark.

I need to move, get to a different tree, but I don't have Finn's agility. If I try, I'll probably end up tumbling straight into the middle of the Sliman horde. All they'd have to do then would be to trample all over me with their heavy boots.

Then the air changes. It's subtle, barely perceptible, but I have no doubt. I *feel* it. The Sliman have inched much closer than I'd have thought possible, and the receptor hasn't sensed it. They've managed to conceal themselves from the device but not from me. It's as if my connection to the receptor has sharpened my intuitive abilities, my instinctive awareness.

I hear rustling noises among the trees about twenty yards away. Finn is sending me a signal. I turn on the receptor, flooding the area around and underneath me with a blinding white light. It will give the Sliman quite an eyeful of my position, but I have to trust that they don't want to kill me, and it will keep them off Finn.

I don't see or hear anything at first, but a moment later the ground trembles and erupts. A handful of Sliman warriors explode from inside the earth, caked in dirt and moving faster than I've ever seen them move before. They managed to tunnel their way to my tree in a matter of minutes.

I whip the receptor toward them. A shockwave blasts them fifty feet into the air, their bodies smashing hard against tree trunks as they crash back down onto the ground.

Finn leaps from his tree, landing in the middle of the next wave of warriors as they surface from the entrails of the earth. He thrusts his knife inside first one and then another Sliman before they even register what's hit them.

Two more are still standing. I calculate my next move, trying to figure out how to strike them without hurting Finn when something tightens around my calf. I barely have time to glance down before I'm yanked from the tree with a vicious force that I cannot match.

Branches snap and twigs claw at my face and arms as I'm dragged down. My left hand scrambles to grab onto anything it can, but my right hand has only one mission: keeping the receptor safe. My whole existence tries to stay focused on this single task, but the shock and pain have almost paralyzed me.

I can't fight it.

Everything the Sliman have done so far has been a decoy. This is the real attack and it's working. I feel helpless and frustrated, and both of those are negative feelings that fail to produce a response from the receptor.

I'm halfway down the tree when the Sliman hand reaches higher, pulls me by the waist and throws me to the ground. I land on my elbow and the pain shoots through me like a poison arrow.

The Sliman who pulled me down looms above me, his glowing green eyes narrowed with purpose. His grip tightens around my leg again, dragging me across the dirt.

I thrash, clawing at the ground, my fingers digging into the damp earth for anything to hold onto.

Finn sees us just as he wrenches his knife from a Sliman's throat. He starts toward us, but another Sliman intercepts him. Finn has no option but to fight him.

I twist around, trying to escape the Sliman's grip. He yanks harder and then lets go of my leg. I glance back to see him loading a tranq gun with gloved hands. The receptor lies just a few yards away. If I close my eyes, I could call it to destroy my attacker, but my fear overrides logic. My hand reaches for my pulse gun instead. I find it in its holster, but my fingers are shaky and can't draw it fast enough.

The Sliman takes a step forward, raising the tranq gun when something massive falls on him and tackles him to the ground—a dark beast larger than he is.

"Shy Boy!"

Relief and disbelief crash through me all at once. *Shy Boy?* How? How did he follow us? How did we not notice?

I lunge for the receptor, pushing past the pain, past the fear. It flies to my hand easily, heating up my palm with a surge of energy. I position it, trying to get a clear shot at the Sliman, but it's not easy. The fight on the ground is a blur of rolling bodies and thrashing limbs. Shy Boy and the Sliman have become an amorphous, shifting mass.

Finn darts past me, launching himself into the chaotic fight of the two huge, dark figures and sinks his knife into the Sliman's chest.

I stand there, breathless, struggling to process what's just happened.

The bodies around us are still. The air is thick with the scent of blood and earth. All the Sliman have been slain or blown to pieces.

And somehow, Shy Boy is here.

I turn, dazed. Finn meets my eyes, his chest heaving. He's risen to the occasion. He has saved Shy Boy, and he has saved me.

I collapse into Finn's arms, overwhelmed. The receptor is still warm in my grasp, but using it still comes at a great cost. Shy Boy lifts me and carries me most of the way back.

CHAPTER 12

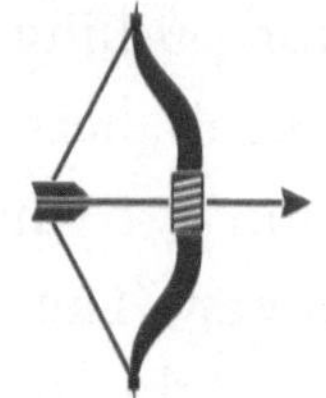

WE SAY GOODBYE TO Shy Boy outside the underground base. He pulls me into a tight hug as he picks at my hair.

"Why did you follow us here, you silly thing? I thought you'd be safe now, spending time with your buddies," I say, hiding my face in his fur. We underestimated the power of his bond with us. I'll have to figure out what to do about this. He needs to be free, away from both humans and Sliman.

Finn opens the trapdoor, and we jump inside, landing softly on our feet. We hurry down the hallway, slowing down as we approach our living quarters. The last thing we need is to wake up everyone.

Finn stops outside my door, but I keep walking. He catches up with me in a few quick strides and grabs my arm. "You're doing this now?" he asks.

"Yes, now. Before he has time to piece together what we've done tonight. You know he'll yell until he turns purple. We have to catch him off guard."

Finn shakes his head but knows better than to try to stop me.

I knock on Damian's door. He opens it almost instantly, and I blink in surprise. His room is lit—he's been up.

His eyes narrow, scanning our disheveled state, trying to make sense of why we're standing at his door at this hour.

"Can we come in?" Finn says.

Damian steps aside to let us in. I take two steps and then freeze on the spot. Zoe is sitting on the bed.

Her eyes widen. "Goodness, what happened to you? You look terrible."

I glance at Finn. His clothes are streaked with mud, and there's caked blood on his hands, not to mention the bruises and cuts all over his face. I imagine I don't look much better. On top of all that, every slight movement of my left arm sends sharp stabs of pain through my elbow.

Fractured, probably. Twisted at the very least.

Damian crosses his arms, his gaze flicking between the two of us. "Yeah, what the hell happened to you? Where have you been?"

"That's why we're here," Finn says. "We need to talk, Damian."

I turn to Zoe. "It's kind of private."

She doesn't get it right away. When it clicks, her eyebrows shoot up. "Really? So private that I can't be part of it?"

Finn shrugs. "It's up to Damian. He can fill you in later if he wants. But for now, all I can say is that I'm following Daphne's instructions."

Zoe springs to her feet. I know she'd give anything to stay and participate in the conversation, but the moment Finn mentions Daphne's name, she exhales and heads for the door, even if it's the last thing she wants to do.

Damian has a hard time processing all this. As soon as Zoe leaves, he grabs Finn's shoulder. "Daphne? What's Daphne got to do with this?" he growls.

"Daphne wanted you to have something after she was gone," I say. "She left Finn in charge of it. We had to go get it for you before the drones arrive."

I was right. He's too stunned to focus on the fact that we sneaked out of the base. He lets go of Finn's shoulder and shifts his attention to me.

"What did she want me to have?" he says, his voice more controlled now. "And why?"

"You know about her premonitions. She told Finn to give you this box if they came true. If she... if she died."

Damian's expression darkens, but he doesn't speak.

"We don't know what's inside the box," Finn says, pulling it out of his pocket and handing it over to Damian.

Damian grips it with the tips of his fingers as if it could burn him.

"Let's go, Freya," Finn says, but I can't move. I need to know what's in that box. It wasn't part of my plan, but now the idea of leaving Damian alone with this burden is inconceivable.

I need to be here.

I need to *see*.

"Let's give him some privacy," Finn insists, taking my left hand. I let out an involuntary cry as searing pain shoots through my elbow again.

Damian's head snaps up. "What's wrong?"

"It's nothing. I hurt my elbow when we were out. Fell out of a tree."

His eyes narrow as he processes this. "What the hell were you doing in a tree?"

"Long story," I mutter. "Can I stay?"

"Freya!" Finn reprimands me.

Damian exhales, running a hand through his hair. "It's okay," he says. "You can both stay."

It occurs to me that he's scared to be alone with the box. I remember Finn saying something like that. It's not what's inside the box; it's memories he's afraid of.

Damian sits at his desk and inspects the small, black box, turning it over in his hands before lifting the lid. He takes out a lock of silky blond hair—*Daphne's hair*. He stares at it for a moment, then sets it on the desk.

Next, he retrieves what looks like a touchpad. It's smaller than the touchpads we use now, probably one of those older models Theo discarded when we took over the alien facilities. All three of us exchange wary glances.

Damian presses the power button. The touchpad works. A soft hum fills the air as it boots up, followed by the familiar static and frequency-searching sounds. Then, the screen flickers to life, and an icon appears.

A message from Daphne.

Finn shifts beside me. "We can go now if you want."

Damian doesn't acknowledge the offer. Instead, his fingers move to the screen. With a slight tap, Daphne's face appears, heartbreakingly alive. Soon afterward, her melodic voice fills the room and our hearts.

Hi Damian.

If you're listening to this, it means that my vision has come true and that I have died in a flood. It also means you're freaking out right now, which you deserve in a way.

If my premonition about dying has been true, then a lot more things that I have sensed might be true as well. I owe you this after all the confusion I've put you through lately.

Where do I start? Let me see... do you remember the night we had to spend in a cave because of the apes? Well, we didn't know it was apes just yet, and we weren't sure about the future. My senses and intuition always sharpen in situations of uncertainty.

At dawn you went out with Freya, and I followed you. I'd already had the premonition of my death and although I didn't want to believe it, it created such intense feelings in me that I was seeing life differently. I started to open up to my psychic skills and let them take over. I was in pain and had a million questions that required answers, but the answers were nowhere to be found.

So I followed you. I don't know what I expected to see, but it was when you stopped walking and locked eyes with Freya that I sensed it. You two are drawn to each other for reasons that I cannot fathom, reasons that go beyond your personal choices or desires. I felt it as clearly as anything I have ever felt. You were born to be placed together somehow. But being together will also bring an incredible amount of grief and disaster for you and everyone around you.

What I foresaw is so grave, so dark that I don't even want to think about it, let alone repeat it. It will be the end of everything you know, everything you have fought for. I know your heart and it is a true heart. But there are things out of your control. You hate the very idea of not being in charge, but you can't do anything about it this time.

Damian, this is not me trying to keep you away from her from the grave, this is me giving you a warning that might save humanity. Stay away from Freya, she's better off with Finn. She probably doesn't even know it yet, but she will come to you. And when she does, you will have to be the one who's strong and send her away. Don't doubt what I'm telling you. For you, for her, for the Saviors, for the Earth, you two have to fight against your fate and stay away from each other.

Tomorrow is the day of the big battle against the aliens. I don't want to visualize it, I don't want to know if it'll be the day that I die, but know that whatever I do, I do out of love for you.

I have asked Finn to help me and he's doing whatever he can, the perfect knight that he is. I've told him everything except for the part where your destiny is intertwined with that of Freya's. You know that Finn and Freya love each other. Let them be. Let circumstance win over fate. Let the human prevail over the alien. For, somehow, I think the aliens have something to do with all this. I can't explain it otherwise.

I have always loved you, Damian. And though I have faded now into the shadows, I love you still.

We all watch as Daphne, our fierce friend, becomes as sweet and vulnerable as a small girl on the screen of the touchpad. I quickly wipe a tear from my cheek before Finn or Damian notice.

After her moment of reflection, Daphne has one more thing to add.

Oh, I should have said this earlier, listen to this message alone.

The screen goes black, and Damian breaks out in laughter. "Typical Daphne," he says. "Saving the most important part for last. When it's useless."

His attempt to evade his broken heart isn't working. His eyes have turned red. His body is shivering. Daphne has always meant a lot to him and to hear her voice like that must have shaken him to the core. I fear the shadows now will always haunt him.

I am frozen. My limbs feel heavy, my head is spinning, unable to process the words we've just heard. I don't dare to look at Finn—I don't want to try and guess what goes through his mind. This is the last thing any of us expected to hear and it's impossible to digest all the implications of Daphne's message.

Damian holds his face with both hands. I'm sorry I had to do this to him, but he left me no choice. Maybe, just maybe one good thing will come out of this. Maybe he will remember it was Daphne he really wanted. Maybe her words will encourage him to stay away from me.

"What do you make of this?" Finn asks in a whisper.

Damian looks at both of us. "She always had a tendency to exaggerate," he says. "She had a vivid imagination. A flair for the dramatic. She believed in her delusions to the point where they killed her." He spews out those last words with indignation and bitterness.

His last line of defense.

But I've had the same thoughts. That Daphne forced her destiny onto herself the way she imagined it. That she acted in a reckless manner because of her faith in her visions. That the tragic result could have been avoided if she hadn't convinced herself she was destined to die.

I don't want to go and leave Damian by himself, but what choice do I have? Choices are taken away from me every time I choose Finn, and I always choose Finn. Tonight is no different.

I try to get up, but my legs feel as if they were made of lead. The pain in my elbow returns with extra viciousness. A well-deserved punishment for my insolence, my arrogance, my manipulations.

When I glance at Finn, I get scared. He looks devastated. His eyes have sunk deeper in their sockets. His beautiful lips, lips as beautiful as any girl's, are dry and chapped. Most alarmingly, his sunny Finn essence has vanished.

I help him up. I squeeze Damian's hand before I go, but he doesn't respond to my touch in any way. There's more of him in my mind now than ever before. How am I going to juggle all these feelings? How am I going to face what's coming next for the Saviors when I'm a mess inside?

Finn walks me back to my room and I want to ask him to stay with me, but I figure it's not fair to him. I've caused him enough trouble and pain for one night.

I feel his hand on mine as I turn the door handle. He wraps his arms around me from behind and kisses my ear.

"I love you, Freya," he says, "whichever way the world turns, I love you."

"Finn, it's not the time—" I start to say, but he hushes me.

He slips away to his room, and I have to enter mine alone.

I lie down on my bed. I seem to float there in a chaotic buzz of abstract thoughts and uncertain pangs of mad love and confusion. One last thought rises before sleep takes my exhausted, worn-out body.

What was Zoe doing in Damian's room so late?

That doesn't matter. Not tonight. Tonight, the only girl that matters lives in the shadows.

CHAPTER 13

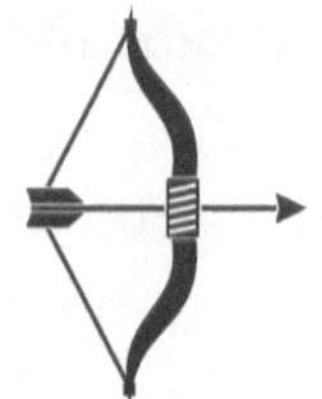

It's impossible to tell day from night in the tunnels, but the distant clatter of knives and forks against metal plates tells me it's probably midday.

Noon!

I throw off the blanket and jump out of bed, regretting it immediately as pain shoots through my elbow.

When I catch my reflection in the mirror, I grow alarmed. I don't know how I'll show my face today.

A big, ugly bruise covers most of my right cheek. Thin scratches stretch across my forehead, my nose and my upper lip. My lower lip is swollen, and the whites of my eyes are laced with broken capillaries. Not to mention how filthy I look. It's as if I've been baked in mud.

I go to the sink and turn the water on with my good hand. I can barely move my left elbow now. I should go straight to Doc about that. He'll fix it. He can fix anything. I just hope it won't interfere with training.

I splash water over my face and arms, but it will take a lot more than that to get the grime and dried blood off my skin. I strip down as quickly as my useless left arm allows me. I discover multiple bruises and lacerations all over my body, my ribs, my arms, my thighs. A fresh, angry cut gashes across my right leg, still sluggishly bleeding.

When did that happen?

I press a wet cloth to the wound, hissing as I wipe away the blood, and slap my last band-aids across the cut. I pull on my only clean clothes. They're old, worn at the seams, but they'll have to do for now. I'll have to ask Wudak later about how laundry works around here.

Wudak. He won't be pleased with Finn and me when he finds out what we did last night, but I think I can handle him. He keeps calling me a queen, doesn't he?

Damian is a different story. I don't even want to imagine what will come out of his mouth once he's had enough time to fully process what transpired last night.

I make my way to Doc's room, hoping he'll be able to patch me up before anyone else sees me, and knock. No answer. *Damn.* After a few more tries, I have to accept that he's not here. It was a long shot anyway.

With a sigh, I walk to the main cavern where the long tables are set up. I'm surprised to find everyone there. The moment they see me, all conversations stop. It feels like they've been waiting for me.

Not good.

Doc raises an eyebrow. "You're in worse condition than Finn," he says. He turns to Finn. "I thought you said she practiced with the receptor? It looks like she's been involved in hand-to-hand combat."

Before Finn can answer, Pip runs over to hug me. "Does it hurt?"

"Just a little bit," I say, doing my best not to let her notice how my left arm dangles from my shoulder.

"What happened, Freya?" Tilly asks. "Why did you two go out last night?"

I have no idea what Finn has told them already, so I look to him for guidance with pleading eyes. Doc has put some kind of powder on the cuts and bruises on his face and Finn looks like a ghost.

"We snuck out to practice like I told you," Finn says. "Just for old times' sake. Before the drones make that impossible."

"And then what?" Rabbit says.

"Then they attacked a whole Sliman Regiment," Wudak announces as he steps in the cavern, armed to the teeth. He's got two shock-bows on his back, two guns and two swords around his waist. He must have just returned from Plantation-15.

"They did what?" Damian says. I'm surprised he hasn't figured it out on his own yet. It's pretty hard to hide anything from him, but Daphne's message must have thrown him off his game.

Wudak looks at me. "How could you, Freya? Has my trust in you been misguided? Have you not heard a word of what I have said to you?"

"It's not Freya's fault," Finn says. "I put this whole thing in motion. It was my idea."

"You're supposed to protect her," Wudak says, looking straight into Finn's eyes. He's angry and frustrated. I haven't seen this side of him yet.

"I'm not a child, I'm responsible for my own actions," I say.

"Clearly, you're not," Wudak says. "Neither of you has a sense of responsibility."

"They won, didn't they?" Damian comes to our defense. This shocks me more than Wudak's reaction. "Two against an entire regiment and they both made it back? I'd say that's pretty impressive."

Wudak is not pleased with any of this. "They have informed the Lagerians of your position. They now know you are still in the district. How is this an impressive development?"

Damian shrugs. "They've known. How could they not after we attacked that convoy? They know we're still in the district. Escaping would be next to impossible with the toxic fumes sealing off the borders. You're angry because your buddies got axed."

Wudak grinds his teeth so loud the sound vibrates

through the cave walls. For a moment, I think he and Damian are about to lunge at each other.

Doc intervenes just in the nick of time. "I need to take care of Freya. That arm of hers is in really bad shape. You two can argue all you want later."

He takes my good arm and leads me to the Labs, where he has set up his brand-new office. Pip follows close, gripping my shirt as if afraid I'll slip away. The Labs combine all the things you'd expect to find in Doc's medical station and Theo's tech lair. Screens and monitors blink with data, microscopes and test tubes clutter the countertops.

Doc gestures to a cot. "Sit."

I ease myself down, wincing at the sharp throb in my elbow. Doc picks up his handheld ultrasonic scanner and runs it over me from head to toe for signs of more serious injuries.

"Where did you get that?" I ask. "I thought you left the one you had back in the camp."

"The Sliman are well equipped," he says as he examines the elbow, pressing gently around the joint.

"Ouch," I protest.

"They have everything I could possibly need here. That elbow's been badly abused but it's not fractured. It's sprained," he concludes, reaching for a sling. "You'll need to keep it immobilized for a few days."

"I don't know if I have a few days. I have to practice using the receptor. I can't focus properly yet, and it's exhausting me. Hence the injuries."

"Uh-huh." He slips my arm into the fabric, adjusting the straps until my forearm rests snug against my torso. The support takes some of the strain off. "That should help," he says, securing the sling in place. "No sudden movements, no lifting, and definitely no fighting—at least for a week."

I give him a flat look. We both know that's not happening.

Doc cleans the cuts on my face and applies the same ghost powder that he put on Finn earlier.

"You look so funny," Pip says.

"Thanks, Pip, that really helps my confidence."

"Well, you're welcome," she says, smiling. She's so innocent and sweet it breaks my heart.

Doc eyes me now. "Freya, do you mind if I draw some blood? I'd like to run some tests."

"Do you think there's any left?" I joke, but Doc doesn't smile. "Blood, I mean." Doc tries again not to smile, but he does, a little. "Doc?"

"I get it, Freya. It's not that funny."

"Is what funny?" Pip asks.

"See?" Doc says.

Okay, maybe I'm not a barrel of laughs.

"It was pretty foolish of you," Doc says, "going out there on your own, and for what?"

"We didn't plan on running into any Sliman guards.

And we wouldn't have if it weren't for the wolf trap."

"Speaking of Sliman, I might as well tell you. We decided this morning that Theo and I will try to analyze and reproduce Omicron 5. If we succeed, and that's a huge if, it will be up to you to bind it with the receptor. If you think it wise, of course, and if these thirty Sliman here truly turn out to be our friends."

I'm gone for one morning and this is what happens. "What did Damian have to say about it?"

"He agreed—for the time being anyway. He said we can't let the Sliman know if we're successful, not until you're in complete control of your receptor."

There is a lot of trust between Doc and Damian. I know that if I drill him enough, he'll give me information about Damian's current state of mind. Information that might be useful to me.

"I'll need to take a look at that cut on your thigh, too," Doc says as he prepares the syringe he will use to draw blood. He points to a gown and turns the other way so I can change.

A moment later, he has the needle inside my vein.

"What are you hoping to find, Doc?"

"I'm not sure. Anything that might give me a clue as to why you are the way you are. Hopefully, I'll understand more about the aliens."

Doc rips the band-aids off the wound on my thigh in one quick motion. I hiss at the sting but bite back a complaint. "I don't see any signs of infection," he says, covering the cut with his healing powder before wrapping it in fresh bandages.

I'm about to press him for more information on Damian when the door swings open and Theo strides in with Zoe and Nya right behind him.

"I should have sent you and Finn straight to Doc last night," Zoe says. Her voice is sad but not reprimanding.

Theo frowns. "You saw them *last night*? I thought they didn't get back until dawn."

Lucky for me, Zoe doesn't seem eager to expand on that. Maybe she knows in her gut there's a lot more to our story than she wants to hear. Instead, she turns to Doc. "Is Freya going to be alright?"

Doc nods with a smile on his face.

"There are two of us now with bandaged thighs," Nya says.

"You had it a lot worse than me."

"Finn just told us everything. How was it?"

"How was what?"

"The fight," she says with a voice tinged with excitement and expectation.

I shake my head. "I thought Finn told you *all* about it." I reach for my clothes, figuring I can change back in my room. The sooner I get out of here, the better.

"Those are in bad shape," Zoe says as she snatches away my clothes. "Come with me, I'll give you some of mine."

"Finn gave us an account of the facts," Nya says as I stand up. "I want to know how it felt. Being out there, just the two of you, against an army. And killing them all."

I shift uncomfortably. "Maybe a few survived," I say, suddenly aware of the stark difference between us. Nya speaks with certainty and conviction. I second-guess everything—every choice, every action—before I can finally settle on a decision.

But as she continues talking about the thrill of smelling your enemy's fear, the urgency of making split-second choices, the weight of knowing your partner's life depends on you, I realize something—it did feel good. It felt good fighting side by side with Finn. Moving as one. Trusting each other completely.

Pip wants to stay in the Labs with Doc, so I follow Zoe to her room. She gives me an earful about how Nya has practically become Theo's shadow.

"I don't know where this sudden interest in him is coming from," she says, tossing a new pair of leather pants, a black t-shirt and a pair of black leather boots onto the bed. "Sometimes I think she does it just to annoy me."

I stare at the clothes in disbelief. All shiny leather. All black. "Why would she want to annoy you? And why would you be annoyed in the first place?"

"I don't know. It's Nya after all. Who knows why she does anything?"

"Okay, but why are you so bothered by what she does?"

Zoe thinks about this. "I don't know that either. I guess I'm a bit territorial when it comes to Theo. It's not like you and Finn. We don't have that kind of connection, but he is like family to me. And Nya is, well, she's kind of dangerous."

I can't help but laugh. "Well, that's good. We need dangerous people in this group. Zoe, you don't seriously expect me to wear these pants."

"I just don't want her to play games with Theo. And put those pants on, they fit you. They're a bit short on me."

"He's not that vulnerable, Zoe. He's a Savior. Don't forget that. Are you sure there's nothing else going on?" I study her face, not sure what I'm looking for. "I'm talking about your feelings."

Zoe shakes her head. "No, it's not like that. He's so carefree and everything is simple to him. If I could ever choose someone to be with, it would be someone complicated enough to keep me interested."

"Like Damian," I say, almost imperceptibly.

"Well, yes, I guess. Like Damian if he wasn't Damian, of course."

Somehow, I know what she means. "Can you keep a secret?"

Zoe nods. "A secret! It's been a while since I heard one. Come on, don't keep me in suspense," she says, rubbing her hands together like a little girl.

"Shy Boy is here. He followed us when we left the camp. He followed Finn and me last night and he practically saved my life."

I give Zoe an account of last night's events. I can tell she's hooked right away. Then she puts two and two together. "You came to find Damian right after you returned to the base. You said it was private. Was it connected to the real reason why you and Finn went back to the camp?"

No matter how you look at it, Zoe deserves to know the truth. At least, the main part. Besides Damian, she was the one person closest to Daphne. So, I tell her about Daphne, about the box she left for Damian, about how Finn felt it was his obligation to deliver it. I leave out the part where I was present when Damian opened the box.

Zoe is stunned. She takes my hand. "I would have gone, too, if I knew." Tears begin to form in her eyes.

I have seen so many tears over the years, yet every time they devastate me. Tears of anger, tears of pain, tears of helplessness and tears of loss. They always resurface, in captivity and in freedom, because to be human is to love and to love often means sorrow.

CHAPTER 14

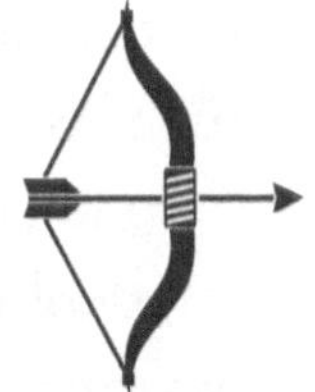

I MOVE THROUGH THE tunnels in Zoe's black leather pants and boots. They help keep me warm against the damp chill of the cavernous space that's become our new home. One week after the encounter with the Sliman regiment, my face has almost returned to normal. The bruises have faded to a barely noticeable faint yellow, and the scratches have healed, leaving behind thin traces of pink.

My elbow is a different story. Doc insists it should be fine by now, but it still feels stiff and sore. Then again, I haven't exactly given it the rest he advised. I've been training with the others for hours each day, pushing through exhaustion like it's the only thing keeping me sharp and sane.

The Sliman don't spend much time at the base. They have to report to the plantations and perform their daily duties. More often than not, we're left completely alone. Wudak only appears every other day, staying just long enough to teach me something new about the receptor—how to control it better, how to unlock another layer of its power. He says I'm making remarkable progress, that the device is taking much less of a toll on my body.

According to Wudak, two alien drones have landed safely so far but haven't been deployed yet.

I've noticed that he's more reserved with me now, more distant. I'm not sure if it's because of my recklessness that night with the Sliman regiment, or if something else is weighing on him. But this morning, when Wudak enters the training ring, his face is clouded with a new kind of concern. He walks straight to me and bows. "It has started," he says.

His words send a ripple through the room. Everyone stops what they're doing. We quickly gather around Wudak.

"The drones launched last night," he continues. "They covered the entire district, including all fifteen plantations, within hours. We don't have hard evidence yet, but we believe the drones are equipped with digital sensors that can track down your sensory receptor device when it's powered." His eyes settle on me. "You're not safe, Freya, not even here. I'm sorry."

"So, moving here was for nothing?" I ask, more than a little frustrated.

"No, of course not. If you hadn't been here last night, they would have you already. But it's not enough. We need to get you out of the district."

I'm trying to wrap my mind around what he has said. We all are.

"We thought it was impossible to move from district to district," Damian says. "Haven't the districts been cut off with wide craters of some kind of toxic mud that will kill you when inhaled or touched?"

"Acidic trimphonites, yes," Wudak says. "They warned you about them in the plantations. They showed you videos of the areas when they exposed animals to the effects of the poison just for the benefit of having you watch. The trimphonites enclose the district of the plantations to keep them safe at all times—though from what nobody knows."

I stare at him. "So?"

"So, it's a lie." He says this with a blank expression on his face, like this simple phrase is all that's needed.

"I'm sorry, what?"

"The trimphonites aren't there to keep things from coming in. They are put there to keep you from getting out. To achieve that, they didn't have to cover the entire perimeter with that nasty stuff that's really hard to come by. Only selective points. Most of the mud is harmless but you wouldn't know it."

"And you know that for sure?" I say.

"We know of at least one safe spot, and we've been moving in and out of the district for years."

"So, you know what's out there?" Rabbit says with dreamy eyes. I half-expect him to ask Wudak if he has seen any cheetahs.

"What *is* out there?" Damian asks. "More plantations? More breeding villages? More Sliman? More terror and death?"

"We only know of the one district that we can reach through the safe passage. There are no plantations there, no villages. No trees and no animals. It's a desert, a dead land. Destroyed by chemical missiles many decades ago. Nothing can grow there, nothing can live."

I shake my head. "But we found a map—"

"We put it there," Wudak cuts me off. "To get you thinking of new possibilities."

Damian folds his arms. "Then why do you go to that district?"

"And why do you want to take Freya to that wasteland?" Finn cuts in.

"Because it's safe. Because it's not surveyed. Because that's where the revolution will begin."

"How am I supposed to live there?" My imagination is already running wild with images of the Sahara and the Gobi deserts, the arid lands I've read about in encyclopedias.

"The crossing point is only a few miles to the west.

Once we cross it, we'll have to travel for another ten miles before we reach Zolkon's fortress."

I remember that name. Wudak mentioned it the first night we arrived at the base when we asked who was behind the construction. The details of who Zolkon is make my head spin as I hear Wudak explain that Zolkon built the underground base and reconstructed the desert fortress. He's a member of the main engineering team for all fifteen plantations—the only Sliman member. He is also the leader of what Wudak calls *the Sliman insurgence*. All the rebel Sliman, including Wudak himself, follow Zolkon's command.

This new information makes Damian even more suspicious. He looks at Wudak for a long while with veins pulsing in his temples. I can't blame him. I'm taken aback myself. This idea of another Sliman leader building fortresses in the desert is a bit hard to swallow.

But then Wudak says something that gives us all pause. "Zolkon believes he can recalibrate the sensory receptor to make it untraceable. When it comes to designing technology, there's nothing he can't do. You'll stay in the fortress as long as it takes for him to complete the recalibration. Once it's done, I'll bring you back, and you'll be ready to train again. I would take the receptor myself, but I know you won't trust me with it."

I exhale, slowly. "We need to think about this."

"Think, then, but understand this—we're running out

of options. It's either that, or the receptor stays powered off permanently. And no one else can go with us. We can't risk drawing unnecessary attention. It will be just you and me on this journey. I'll return in the evening. I hope you'll have an answer for me by then."

❖

DAMIAN APPROACHES ME IN the training ring as I wipe the white sticky powder from my hands. The Sliman gave it to us—it keeps our palms free of sweat when handling weapons. I'm the last one to leave the ring before lunch. I'm afraid to stop moving, because then I'd start thinking.

"I talked to Wudak two days ago," Damian says.

I glance at him. I'm surprised, and he knows it. That was probably his intention.

"I asked him about a lot of things, and he gave me more answers than I expected," he says, sounding sincerely impressed. "I hate to admit it, but he seemed almost honest. Either that, or he's rehearsed his lies so well they sound real."

I frown. "What did you ask?"

"The big questions. What happens when we're taken from the plantations. Where they take us. What the life expectancy is after the transfer."

I already know the answer, but I ask anyway. "Were any

of his answers hopeful?"

He shakes his head. "Wudak doesn't have all the details. Far from it. He says no Sliman has a complete picture. Not even this Zolkon apparently. But here's the gist of it. When children show no potential for genetic enhancement, they're either sent off to the breeding villages or shipped to the mines overseas, as Wudak put it. He's never seen them, but he's heard rumors that the aliens are searching for remnants of primitive meteorites that fell there centuries ago."

My entire body stiffens. "Why?"

"They think those meteorites contain certain radioactive isotopes that could hold the key to the recovery of the alien species."

I stare at him, troubled. "You should run this by Theo."

"I will. Once I come to terms with the fact that kids sent to the mines aren't expected to last longer than a year. Two, if they're lucky."

He sinks onto the hard, cold floor of the ring, hiding his face in his hands. I hesitate for a moment, then sit beside him.

"It gets worse," he says. "The ones that do show potential, the ones like us ironically, they're shipped off to planet Sliman, another world the Lagerians invaded and enslaved the indigenous population just like they did on Earth."

"The planet where the first Sliman came from. Where

they were first genetically modified," I say as it dawns on me.

"Yes. The children there are turned into guinea pigs. The aliens run multiple experiments on them in search of an answer. Most of them die in agony. All alone. Desperate. Some are turned into slaves. Some are executed just for the fun of it. Wudak doesn't know what happens to those that survive the experiments."

He slams the floor hard, and I have to grab his hand to stop him from doing it again. When he turns his face to me, there are tears in his eyes.

"Who is it?" I say as it hits me. "Who is it that you've lost?" The truth is I know nothing about Damian—nothing about his life before the Saviors or before Plantation-2. We have all opened up at one time or another, but not Damian.

"Too many to remember. It doesn't matter. They're all dead."

I know his despair because I have felt it. It has cut through my flesh and bones. It has made me angrier, but it hasn't made me stronger.

"You should go," he says. "You should meet that Zolkon character. We have to fight, and we can't win without you and the receptor. It's a risk worth taking."

I nod. I know he's right.

"And I will go with you."

"No, you won't."

"I will."

"Wudak would never let you of all people go. He can't stand the sight of you," I joke.

"What about you? Can you stand the sight of me? Or are you too scared to even think about me after what Daphne said in that recording?"

I'm not sure why I thought we'd never have this conversation. I don't want to mull over Daphne or her dark prophecies. I've managed to avoid thinking about the recording altogether. Like a virus or a poison, I've expelled it from my system with medicinal doses of sleep. I've been going to bed early and getting up late. I can't remember when the last time was that I slept so deeply and soundly as I have this past week.

I don't want to talk about it, and yet I'm drawn to this moment of sincerity that I share with Damian. It's been such an emotional time ever since Finn and I fought the Sliman regiment—ever since I kissed Finn for the first time. Ever since Damian and I started arguing about the imaginary relationship we could have. I want life to be simple again. Sleep, eat, practice, laugh and learn.

"I don't believe what Daphne said. I don't believe in destiny," I tell him. "I don't believe in dark forces that control people as if we were puppets in a play."

"What about the aliens? She said they were involved somehow."

"Nobody can control people's feelings," I insist. "Not

even the aliens. To assume that is to admit we are powerless, and we are not. Look how much we've achieved against all odds."

"Conviction becomes you," he says with a half-smile.

"If we could always be like that."

"Decent to each other?"

"I was going to say nice, but yes, decent works, too."

He springs to his feet but then changes his mind. He squats back down and brings his face close to mine. "I cared about Daphne," he says. "You know that. It's bad enough she's gone, but to know she did it to save me has been a tremendous burden." He looks into my eyes with the deepest sincerity. "I will try and work through this, Freya."

The fragility in his voice almost breaks me. When he goes, I realize that he's given me permission to leave with Wudak, and at the same time he's eased my conscience about forcing Daphne's secrets on him. Damian is an ocean whose depths I may never manage to fathom completely.

CHAPTER 15

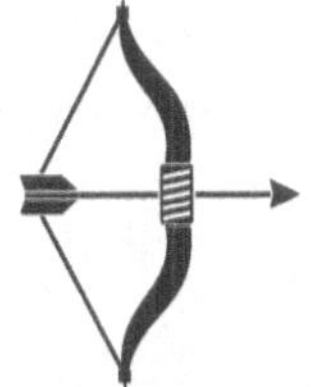

BISCUIT RUNS THE UNDERGROUND kitchen with impressive efficiency. He's transformed the space into something entirely his own. He bakes batches of bread rolls and cookies daily, setting half of them aside for when the Sliman guards return. With the supplies they leave on his counter, he makes beef stew and chicken casseroles—dishes we hadn't tasted in a long time.

The kitchen is a small cave at the end of a long hallway, one of the only places in the base, besides the Labs, with a steady supply of electricity. The fridge hums, and the oven stays warm, keeping this space more alive than the rest of the tunnels.

A sturdy counter sits in the center with shelves underneath that are neatly stacked with pots and dishes. A small metallic table with a few chairs is pushed to the side.

I watch Biscuit as he spreads flour on the counter before

unfolding the dough and kneading it one last time.

"Do you want to help?" he asks me.

"No, thanks. I could never match your skill."

He nods. "You're probably right."

"You're not supposed to say that, Biscuit," I protest. "You're supposed to say I can do anything just as good as you."

"Of course, you can. Well, not everything. I don't think you could ever smell out a rhubarb bush among thousands of shrubs and then make a rhubarb pie."

"No, I couldn't, and I'm kind of grateful for that."

I have a hard time reconciling the two Biscuits in my mind—the one seeking some sort of domestic bliss in every kitchen and the one that plunges into battle with unparalleled bravery and skill.

Rabbit and Scout stroll into the kitchen, side by side. Seeing them like that, I realize just how much Rabbit has grown. He's at least two inches taller than he was three months ago, and he's filled out, no longer the scrawny boy he used to be. Life in the underground base has been hard on all of us, but especially on Rabbit. Not being able to run makes him antsy and restless, always fidgeting, always on edge. Maybe that's why he's been eating more.

"We're starving," he announces, heading straight for the fridge.

"When are those going to be ready?" Scout asks, eyeing the rolls Biscuit is expertly shaping with the dough.

She reaches out to grab some dough, but Biscuit slaps her hand away. "You have to say *please. A*nd about an hour," he says.

Scout scrunches up her nose. "Please," she says imitating Biscuit's voice. "And an hour is too long."

"There's breadsticks in the fridge," Rabbit says, grabbing one and tossing it to her.

"You're supposed to heat them up first," Biscuit says, rolling his eyes.

"I like them better cold," Rabbit says with a shrug, taking a big bite.

I lean against the counter. "Where's Tilly?"

"She'll be here soon. She's with Wudak in the ring," Scout says. "Well, everyone is. We just got tired."

Rabbit grins. "And hungry."

I straighten immediately like I've been electroshocked. "Wudak's back?"

Rabbit nods. "Yeah. He brought Gritu and Malzod with him."

An uneasy feeling settles in my stomach. Why didn't Wudak call for me? I need to talk to him. I need to give him my decision.

Without another word, I turn and head toward the training ring.

Wudak is training with Finn, Nya, Tilly and Theo. Damian and Doc watch the action with their backs against the wall and with Pip sitting at their feet. On the opposite wall, Gritu and Malzod are busy cleaning their pulse guns.

"The main issue that the primitive Sliman have is the one that the Lagerians have as well," Wudak says. "They don't think they can be defeated. Even now that they know what you kids can do, they still don't think you have a chance in hell. And it has never crossed their minds that there could be a mutiny in the ranks of the mutant army. That's our advantage. That and Freya," he adds as he takes notice of me.

"Well, that's a scary thought," I say, barely able to offer a tiny smile.

The smile of a person who has nothing to be happy about.

Pip gives me one of her biggest smiles, and I know immediately that's not true. I have things to be happy about, plenty of things to fight for.

"I've made my decision," I say. All eyes are set on me now. "I will go with you to Zolkon's fortress, but not because there is no other choice. I will go because it is *my* choice. Because I cannot forget who we are, or what I'm supposed to be. I'm ready to learn, Wudak. Ready to fight. And I trust you."

"Very well," Wudak says, a pleased grin on his face. "Nice to see the daring and confident Freya is back."

"There's a lot I need to learn. I realize that. But I'm also the only one who can do all those things. I won't take this responsibility lightly. We will fight the aliens and we will find a way to keep you alive."

It feels good to say those things, to hear myself say them. Tomorrow I might be doubtful again, but this moment is filled with clarity and certainty.

"The receptors require absolute unison of mind and body. The aliens are losing that ability. You, Freya, have a tremendous amount of energy in you. Never doubt yourself. I will serve you with my life," Wudak says.

"The story of the princess and the frog," Gritu says. Nobody knows how to respond to that.

"Don't you mean Beauty and the Beasts?" Nya says.

Gritu shrugs. "I haven't watched that one."

"You've been watching movies?" Finn asks.

"Yes, at the library, like you."

"Not all of us," Malzod clarifies. "Just him."

"You've known about the library," Damian says.

"We removed the sensors from the library area about a year ago. That's when we first spotted you. We've been trying to figure what to do with that knowledge ever since," Wudak says.

So, my suspicions have been right. Maybe my instincts are spot on when it comes to Wudak, and the receptor as well.

"We leave in the morning," Wudak says. "There's no time to lose."

⟡

Damian catches up to me on my way to my room. It's time to start preparing, physically and emotionally, for what lies ahead. Finn promised to come by after helping clean up the training ring. I need all the help I can get.

"You're doing the right thing," Damian says.

"It really helped talking to you earlier, Damian. Somehow, it made everything clearer, like the night after I realized what I could do with the receptor. Only this time, I don't have to feel guilty about it."

We reach my door and it's obvious he wants to come in.

"Finn will be here soon," I tell him, immediately regretting it. Totally the wrong thing to say. Damian always acts like there's some kind of competition between them, even when they're supposed to be working together.

He pushes the door open, ignoring me, and steps inside first. "There are a few things we need to go over before you leave," he says. "I need you to gather as much information as you can about the fortress and about that Zolkon guy."

"I will, but I hope I won't have to stay long."

He doesn't seem to hear me. "That thing you told me the other day, about using the receptor telepathically. Have you made any progress?"

"Yeah, I guess. I can use it from a distance."

"Good." He nods. "Practice tonight before you go. And demand that you're in the room when Zolkon works on the receptor."

"I know, Damian. You don't need to worry."

"But I do worry. I know it's a necessary step, but part of me feels like we're sending you straight into a wolf's den."

"There's no wolf that can stop me, Damian. Not even you. Now go, I have things to do."

I almost have him out the door when Finn shows up. They stare at each other for a moment, then Damian pulls me by the waist and plants a quick kiss on my lips. I shove him back, but there's no need for that. He's already letting go.

"Is this little show for my benefit?" Finn says under his breath.

Damian grins. "You're the showman, Finn. Funny guy and all. I was just saying goodbye."

"Stop it, both of you." I glare at Damian. "This is not the time or place for your stupid little games. Just go."

He doesn't argue. He just saunters off with a smug smile on his face.

"I wonder," Finn says as we sit on the floor. "Have any of the things Daphne said even registered in his brain?"

"Please, don't tell me that you believed what Daphne said."

"I don't know, but she had a point. He's drawn to you."

"And that will bring about the end of the world as we know it?"

"Yeah, I know. That part's a little cuckoo." He runs his fingers through my hair. "I'm going to miss you, Tick. Promise me you'll be careful."

"Of course I will."

He leans in, but I press my hand over his mouth before he can kiss me.

"Finn, no. I don't think I can handle any more emotions for one day."

We embrace and just sit there, holding each other for a few moments before he leaves to give me time to prepare before dinner.

I pull out the receptor and turn it over in my hands, examining every line and groove.

"You are going with me on a journey," I say. "Serve me well."

CHAPTER 16

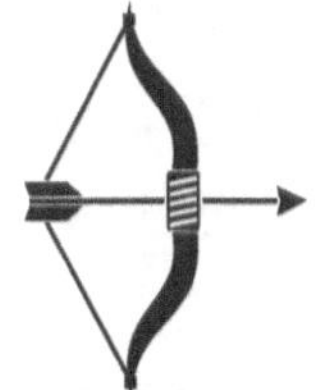

I TIDY UP THE room as best I can, and even though a part of me knows it doesn't really matter, deep down, there's always the fear that I might not be coming back. If that happens, I want to leave a good impression behind, not that of disorder and negligence as if I never cared about anything.

I stack the books I borrowed from the library room on the desk. I fold my clothes, scrub the few dishes in the sink, and sweep the floor with the broom I got from Quax. I smooth out the blanket on the bed and polish my boots until they shine.

When I step back and take in the space, I shrug. It's not a place that anyone would call a home, but it's been some sort of shelter for the past few weeks. I figure it's dinnertime.

With a sigh, I walk to the door, open it and find Damian standing outside.

"What are you doing?" I ask as I check the hallway for witnesses.

"Was just about to knock."

"Haven't we exhausted all subjects already?"

"There's one more thing. Last one, I promise. And it can't wait."

"Ok, come in. But if you're lying—"

"I'm not."

I notice that he has to lower his head to step through the door, and I feel like I've been living in a dwarf's cave all this time.

"You cleaned up," he says as he looks around.

"Just keeping busy on the eve of doom," I say, shrugging.

"You have a premonition the fortress will bring about our doom?"

"What? No, I'm just, you know, making small talk."

He opens his mouth as if he's about to say something. He stops, clears his throat and starts again. "Your Finn hasn't told you the whole truth about what Daphne said to him."

"My Finn?"

"Isn't that what it all comes down to with you? He's your Finn no matter what he says or does, no matter who ends up getting hurt."

"If you came here to berate Finn again, you can save your breath. I'm not interested," I say and walk to the door.

"Your attachment to him is pathetic, blind," he spews out.

I turn back and consider his words, trying to figure out where he's coming from with all this. "It would take you an eternity to understand what Finn and I share. You don't know how to do true friendship."

"Finn didn't tell you the whole truth," he starts all over as he sits on my desk chair. Now at least I'm a bit taller than him.

I wish he would stop with all this already. I know I am to blame for giving him the damned box, but I really can't hear one more word about it.

"The truth about what, Damian? Daphne? Haven't we been over this already? Isn't it painful enough as it is? All three of us heard what she had to say. Why are you bringing it up again? What does it matter now?"

"Because you're leaving. Because I don't know when or even *if* I will see you again. You've told me yourself that any of us could vanish at any moment. Die, get captured, whatever. So, back to your question. I'm telling you because you need to know."

I sigh. "Okay, I give up, tell me. What is the truth?"

"Daphne didn't hate you; she didn't even dislike you. She actually thought there was something special about you. But she was jealous of you, and it started long before she had her premonitions."

I don't know how to take this. So, I smile. "Hmm, that's a very interesting theory, but a bit on the crazy side, to be honest. I mean, how do you even come up with a thing like that? Do you remember the way I used to be? Who would be jealous of that useless creature?"

"I told her I loved you," he says without blinking an eye.

If his intention was to catch me off guard, it has worked. This tone of ambiguity in his voice is nothing new. I've felt it many times before. I don't know if he's joking, if he's serious, if he's playing me. All I know right now is that I want him to continue.

"You told Daphne that you loved me?" I ask in a robotic voice.

"Yes."

"Why?"

"Because I needed to break things off with her. And because it was pretty much true."

I feel like I need to sit down. "Pretty much? Damian, honestly, what's wrong with you?"

"What's wrong with me? The fact that I love you means there has to be something wrong with me?"

"Well, yes. And you can't *pretty much* love someone. I get it now, you're like me. You were afraid of Daphne coming on so strong. You created an affection for me to deflect her," I say, shaking my head. "And then you got stubborn, or competitive, and wanted me because I was out of your reach. You started to believe you wanted me. And then it just became about your competition with Finn."

He glances at me, stunned by this new idea. His sheepish expression means I hit on something true.

"That's just great, Damian. You had a chance at love and you ran, using me as an excuse to get out of it," I say, exasperated.

He shakes his head with a new determination in his eyes. "No. You're wrong again. I told her the truth. She was jealous of you anyway. She made me nervous, looking for clues everywhere and it made her life miserable. She said she needed the truth, Freya."

"So you created one for her," I say, rubbing my temples. "So she would stop making you nervous. I'd be disappointed in you, Damian, but I might have done it myself."

"Is that all you have to say?"

"Seeing myself in you as I just have, now I don't trust anything either of us might say. Daphne and Finn are pure, and they know how to love. The two of us, we are too afraid of that burden."

Once again, I don't see it coming. I should have after all the stunts he's pulled, but I'm too preoccupied trying to figure out what he's set out to accomplish. He grabs me by the waist and when he pulls me closer for a kiss, I punch him hard in the nose.

It barely fazes him physically, but emotionally I see a sudden pause in his passion. It's like he is awakening. Have I finally reached him?

"Yeah, okay," he whispers to himself, not so much defeated as resigned.

He pulls away and walks for the door. I feel the burden of the truth he is now confronting. I know I'm usually like him, avoiding such burdens.

"Damian," I say as he stops with his hand on my door. "She's still out there in the shadows. She will know you love her."

He continues out the door. It's as if he can't hear me anymore.

I should find clarity in this empty room now, but I was revealed as much as Damian. We are emotional cowards unlike Finn and Daphne. We are not to be trusted and so I now feel closer to Damian than ever before. I feel his hurt and I know how he cannot trust his own heart. We are alike. This has been our bond. We are emotional brutes, and he is a physical one as well. His brutishness has drawn me in at times and I like the way he kisses me.

Here I go again. Is there no end to my madness? This journey could not begin too soon. I want to escape Damian and Finn. If only I could escape myself as well.

❖

THE DINING HALL IS quiet. Damian is here and so is Finn. They are much quieter here than they are in my heart. There's also Biscuit, Tilly and Doc. We exchange a few words, and everyone seems to be at ease. This is not what I expected. Everything seems so normal. My great revelation did not tilt the world off its axis.

I consider apologizing to Damian or Finn, or both, but that would take courage, and I don't have it right now.

Wudak walks in the room with Gritu and Malzod and, thankfully, saves me from my poisonous thoughts.

◈

I DON'T GET A chance to approach Damian until after dinner. He walks slowly down the hallway, checking something on his touchpad.

"Damian, I just wanted to say—"

His severe expression stops my lips cold. "I know I don't deserve it, but can we never speak of this again?"

I nod and go to my room. This must be the longest day of my life. All my belongings are placed in my backpack. There's so little that I own, so little that I need. I can move from place to place as easy as a migrant bird. And I don't even have to build a nest.

Some day the blue skies will open up and I won't have to hide anymore. I will fly to all the continents and oceans of the world. Then I will make a home somewhere and fill it up with small belongings that will remind me of every little time, every place and every person that has ever meant something to me.

But maybe it will never happen for us. We can hope for those that will come after us, the next generation of Saviors. Because what we have started will not die out. There will be more and more rebels, more fights and more victories. All I have that makes sense is this fight.

And maybe I will die in battle or maybe I will be captured and turned into an alien incubator. They would not win even then. I would kill myself before I would help them repopulate. Maybe Wudak and I will be ambushed tomorrow and take our last breath in the land beyond the mud.

Maybe I will never see my friends again.

I know there is no one destiny or one answer in front of me. In reality, there is only one answer always. The one that we are willing to give.

I turn on my touchpad and check the time. It's almost midnight. The time for ghosts and those who can't sleep to haunt the world with their heavy eyes. I step out of my room on tiptoes. If I regret this in the morning, so be it. There are a few things that can only be said at night.

I knock on his door, but he doesn't answer. I could turn and go now and forget the whole thing but instead I open the door. I don't want to be a coward anymore. He's wide awake, sitting on the bed.

"You didn't answer," I say.

"One last chance for you to walk away."

"You don't love me. You're like me. You don't know how to love." My voice breaks even as I say this.

He lowers his head so I can't see his eyes when he talks. "All I have ever done is try to protect you. Haven't you seen that? Since that first night at the plantation when I carried you back to safety." He raises his head and looks into my eyes. "You were right. I did love Daphne. How could I not? I was afraid, but now I just feel broken, and you are the only one who understands me. You always have been."

I go to him, I put my arms around his neck and caress his hair right where his tattooed number is hidden. I can almost feel the digits through my fingers. Those painful engravings that bond us all together in misery.

"You're so beautiful, Freya," he whispers. "So frail. So strong."

I kiss him because I want him to know that this is what I want. This is what I choose. Not because he asked but because it's my truth as well at this moment. His skin is warmer than a cat's fur. I touch his burning eyelids and whisper in his ear that we have both suffered more than enough.

CHAPTER 17

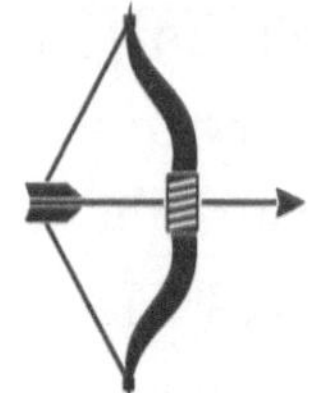

As far as the eye can see to the east and to the west, there's mud and more mud. Thick, sticky, reeking brown and green mud. The crater looks at least a hundred feet wide and we have no choice but to walk through it.

I eye the sludge warily. "How deep is it?"

"Up to your thigh, probably," Wudak says as he steps in. His boots sink with an awful squelch. "It's not quicksand, we can cross."

That doesn't make me feel any better. The thought of dipping my feet and legs inside this viscous mass is less than appetizing. I put my right hand over my nose and mouth to diminish the sense of stench even by the tiniest amount. I take the first step, then the second, watching my boots disappear under the sludge.

I follow Wudak's steady path slowly, trying to ignore the increasing feeling of nausea in my stomach.

I tell myself to stay focused on the opposite side of the mud. Stay focused on the plan.

This morning, before we left, Pip told me to stay strong. Saying goodbye to my friends was harder than I imagined. They escorted me out of the tunnels and stood in the morning light for the first time in weeks.

Pip held on to my hand, refusing to let go until the very last moment. She only let go when Zoe pulled me into a hug.

"Take care," Zoe said. "I'll see you in a few days."

I squeezed her hand and kissed her cheek, feeling grateful for her friendship.

Now, hours later, I'm in the mud all the way to my knees. Wudak turns back every now and then to make sure I'm fine. I wish I'd have had time to talk with Zoe before I left. I have never needed a girlfriend more than now. There's so much I'd like to say to her. So much that I could not tell anyone else.

Tilly had tears in her eyes when she wished me a safe journey. "We will take care of Pip," she promised.

"I know you will. I leave her in excellent hands," I said, hugging Scout.

"Make sure you come back soon, Freya," Rabbit said.

"I'll do my best."

Biscuit gave me a loaf of bread. "With cinnamon," he said. "Your favorite."

I want to reach inside my backpack and get that loaf

out now. Cinnamon bread and some cool water would appease my stomach and quell the nausea, but I don't dare to even blink, for fear I might slip deeper into the mud, hair and all.

Doc patted me on the back. "You're healed," he said. "You're in top shape. Your blood sample was beautiful. I'll have some answers when you return."

I nodded and hugged him. "Don't forget to get some rest every now and then, Doc. You can't work all day and most of the night."

"I can't make promises, but I will try," he said.

Nya gave me one of her smallest bows and a single feathered arrow, which surprised me and almost brought me to tears. She's possessive of her weapons and even sleeps with them.

She hugged me roughly as she whispered in my ear, "There's a hidden explosive mechanism in the arrow. It's small and it won't bring down a building, but it will create plenty of confusion. Use it if you must."

I nodded and kissed her cheek. She scowled immediately—definitely not her thing—and shoved Theo, who was standing behind her, straight into me.

"I'm sorry," Theo muttered, stepping back. "You have to ask Zolkon for some kind of manual on the receptor. I can't touch it without some indication as to how it works."

I promised him I'd do my best. As much as he loves

gadgets, this one fascinates him the most—the one only I can control.

Wudak's voice snaps me back to the present. "Wait."

I freeze mid-step. He reaches into the sludge and digs out a snake. It's covered in mud, making it impossible to tell what kind it is, but I don't need to know. I let out a terrified cry. "Snakes! The one thing I can't stand!"

"The *one* thing?" Wudak says.

I roll my eyes. All men can be jerks, mutants or not.

Wudak examines the snake, turning it in his hands as if it's a harmless twig. "Not venomous," he concludes, tossing it several yards away. The snake lands in the mud with a splat, then vanishes.

I swallow hard. "Do you think there are more?"

"Probably. I always find a couple when I cross the mud."

That doesn't sound good. Not good at all. I slow down—each step causes anxiety. I strain to see through the mud, but it's useless. It's mud after all, not glass. I focus on movement instead, but that's no help either—the surface ripples lazily behind Wudak's legs, making it impossible to tell if something is shifting beneath.

"Come on," he says. "No stalling, we're already behind schedule."

Behind schedule. That's what Theo said earlier when we were saying our final goodbyes. "We're behind schedule regarding you-know-what concerning you-know-whom, so any clues you can bring back will be helpful."

Doc nodded in agreement—obviously, they were talking about Omicron 5, but what kind of clues could I possibly find for them? I'm literally *clueless* when it comes to scientific matters. I don't understand half of what Theo talks about.

"Do you have to be injected with Omicron 5 on the same day every month?" I ask Wudak.

"Yes."

"Have you ever had to wait longer?"

"Once."

Clearly, I'll have to drag the answers out of him. "How long? Did you feel any different?"

"Just one day. And it was nasty. Everything felt different. Watch out, it's deeper here."

He guides me to the left, so I don't step into the hole like he did. I'm much shorter than him and the mud would have gotten up to my waist.

I don't bother covering my nose anymore. The smell doesn't bother me as much now—my mind is elsewhere.

I dreaded the moment I would have to say goodbye to Finn. He came to me with a big, radiant smile on his face. His bluish-green eyes were softer than usual and full of encouragement.

I couldn't find words to make the moment easier. I just hugged him with all my might and held on to him for as long as I could.

"It's only a few days," he said. "Then you'll come back to us."

I smiled but really felt like crying. Finn has this effect on me. He makes me see how much better he is than me—than any of us. How much better I could be.

He placed both hands on my shoulders and kissed my forehead, completely unaware that I'm going to break his heart one day.

The thought hits me hard and I stumble, my foot sinking too fast into the sludge. I barely manage to keep from tumbling over as I lose my balance for a moment. Wudak's hand steadies me back on my feet.

We're halfway through the muddy crater. A vast emptiness of grey and black lies ahead on the other side—boulders, rocks, dust, debris and desolation stretching endlessly in every direction. Even the sky looks sick.

As hard as it was to say goodbye to Finn, saying goodbye to Damian was even harder. He awkwardly stayed at a safe distance as he repeated his instructions from the past twenty-four hours. *Don't leave the receptor out of your sight, don't trust anyone, don't think Sliman are your friends.* Then he pulled me into a quick hug before stepping aside to let me have my final moments with Pip.

Pip's strength surprised me. She didn't cry; she didn't even look sad. "I'm so happy to be with you again, Freya," she said, smiling up at me. "I love you."

That's when the tears came at last, no matter how hard

I tried to hold them back. Wudak and I set off, and for the first time since Plantation-8, I found myself without a single Savior by my side.

I turned my head back, stealing a glance at them one last time. Damian towered over everyone, unmoving, watching. He and I had said our goodbyes hours ago, before the break of dawn, when I had to pull myself away from his arms and return to my room. It was a very hard thing to do, and he didn't make it any easier.

He held onto my hand as I laced up my boots with the other. Just as I reached for the door, he pulled me back and kissed me.

"I'll never leave if you don't stop," I complained in a whisper, half teasing, half pleading, but the thought seemed to amuse him.

"And that's a bad thing?" he said.

"Be serious. I need to sleep, and I can't sleep next to you. I don't want anyone finding out like this."

"You mean Finn."

"I mean anyone. Especially Wudak. I'd never hear the end of it."

He finally let go of me, but I'm still in his arms. He's been in my thoughts ever since. He knows that I chose him over Finn last night, and I'm not sure it was a choice I should have made, but I'm done with regret.

"Here we are," Wudak says. "Final steps."

He takes my hand to help me climb onto the elevated

shore. A few dried-out bushes cling to the cracked earth on the bank, but beyond them, the land is barren. The only spots of shade are occasional huge boulders scattered across the desert floor.

We've made it this far without any danger. We sit down to drink and eat a few morsels before we cover the last ten miles. Cinnamon bread has never smelled or tasted better.

❖

THE FORTRESS RISES BEFORE us like a mirage, something that shouldn't be here. A stolen look into a different world. It's been designed to look like a medieval castle, complete with towers, turrets and thick stone walls reinforced with metal, looming high enough to give you a sense of vertigo if you stare too long.

"This is massive," I say, glancing at Wudak. "I don't get it, how is it possible the aliens don't know about it?"

"Oh, they know about it. They're the ones who commissioned Zolkon to build it."

I come to a sudden halt, my pulse spiking.

Wudak senses my alarm and quickly shakes his head. "No, let me finish. The fortress was built a very long time ago, back when Zolkon was still a young man, but the project was abandoned soon after it was finished. Zolkon has built an energy field around the fortress, shielding any trace of life inside from detection."

"Why did the aliens build it in the first place?" I say, still feeling thrown off by all this.

"Nobody knows. You have to understand, the Lagerians see us as nothing more than slaves—they use us, give us orders, tell us only what is needed and that is that. They never explain their reasons to us."

I try to imagine what Finn would have told me if he were here, how he would piece together the logic behind all this. But it's too late for speculation. We are standing in front of the gates and Wudak announces our arrival through a speaker on the wall.

CHAPTER 18

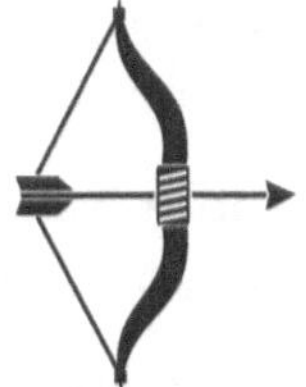

THE HEAVY STEEL GATES open with a groan. We walk through a dark corridor and then come out to a courtyard paved with stone. The different buildings that make up the fortress stand around the courtyard in a circle.

Wudak leads me up a staircase. When we reach the top, we walk across some sort of balcony and then go through a wooden door. We enter a bright circular room with long windows. Wudak points to the largest window in the back of the room. Through its stained glass I see a gigantic, beautiful garden down below, a garden like none I have seen before—not even in my dreams.

There is a water fountain in the middle with many different paths around it that lead to a wide variety of blossomed flowers, most of which I couldn't name. The plants get taller in the distance until they turn into trees.

"I thought you said nothing can grow here," I say.

"So, you were fooled. It's not real. The plants are synthetic. One of Zolkon's many tricks."

We step out of the room and walk around the balcony until we reach another door. This one leads to a hallway with four doors on each side and a bigger one in the back.

"I imagine you are tired," Wudak says. "I'll let you change and rest in the room that has been prepared for you. I'll come and get you when dinner is served."

He opens the first door to the right and ushers me in. The shock that hits me when I cross the threshold can only be compared to the shock of discovering I could use the sensory receptor.

This room is nothing like I expected. There's a huge bed in the middle with a silvery ceiling canopy, a plush sofa and two elegant armchairs by a coffee table with hardcover books stacked on its glass top.

The fireplace is already burning, casting shadows on the lush carpet.

I turn slowly, taking it all in.

Two white doors lead to a bathroom and a large walk-in closet. The bathroom is a marble sanctuary with a big soaking tub surrounded by mirrors reflecting the warm glow of the room.

It's overwhelming. Luxurious. Unreal.

On the counters, sleek metal tools are arranged in a row, looking more like torture instruments than anything else.

I frown and pick one up, then another, reading the

small tags attached to them. "Hair dryer... curling iron... eyelash curler."

"What am I supposed to *do* with these?" I ask, turning to Wudak.

He looks just as lost as I feel. He studies them for a moment, then shakes his head. "Ignore them for now. I'll find out."

With that, he leaves me standing in the middle of this strange, opulent wonderland, completely unsure of what to make of it.

Clearly, this is not what I had envisioned when we set out on our journey. This is not what I imagined I would find when Wudak started talking about the wasteland upon which the fortress was built. I walk around aimlessly unable to calm myself down. I've been going from change to change for so long now I never know what the new day will bring.

I get out of the muddied pants, put on the only other pair I've brought along, and hide the receptor under the pillow. When Wudak comes knocking on the door, I've just managed to doze off. His voice calling my name takes on the form of a headache. I slowly open my eyes. "Come in."

He's holding two huge plastic bags and hands them over to me as soon as I get to my feet. "A present from Zolkon," he says with clenched teeth. "He thought you'd like to try them on for dinner."

It's obvious he doesn't like whatever is in the bags, but he leaves before I have a chance to ask the reason for his reaction.

I dump the contents of the bags onto the bed and scratch my forehead. A present from Zolkon? Seriously? What did he do—go shopping at the *Wasteland Mall?*

I've never seen a dress and shoes like this outside of old photos and movies. It's white and long with delicate straps around the shoulders. Tiny, shimmering beads adorn the front, and a white rose sits at the waist. The shoes match the dress perfectly, white, beaded, elegant.

This can't be real.

In one of the bags, I find a small golden box. I open it cautiously, half expecting an explosive mechanism. Instead, I find a necklace and a pair of earrings, along with lipstick and eye shades.

At the bottom of the box, there is a note.

I hope you will enjoy these small trinkets from past times. Have a bubble bath, have fun getting dressed, and come find us in the big room at the back of the hallway. That's where we'll dine.

About the hair dryer...plug it in and let the warm air dry your hair.

Zolkon

I stare at the note, then at the dress, then at the ridiculous, glittering shoes. A *hair dryer.* The words tug at something buried in my memory—an image from an old magazine or a movie.

I want to call Wudak and ask if this is a joke. How could it not be? Who plans wars and leads rebellions while lounging in silk and pearls? I'm here to have the receptor readjusted, because our lives depend on it. I know this.

And yet... Yet, the fabric feels impossibly soft and fragrant. I twist the lipstick open and apply a thin layer of deep red color over my lips. I walk to the bathroom where I find brushes and combs in the drawers. The bathtub gleams under the dim lighting, already calling to me. I twist the hot water on and watch the bubbles rise. I can pretend to be somebody else just for a little while.

I remember Damian's warning to never let go of the receptor, so I go and retrieve it from under the pillow and place it next to the bathtub, within arm's reach. I let myself sink into the hot bubbly water, feeling how the warmth soothes the stiffness in my muscles instantly.

Afterward, when I look in the mirror with the white dress and matching shoes on, my brown hair falling in soft curls over my shoulders and down my back, and the silver necklace resting against my collarbones, I have a hard time recognizing the girl who stands there with a smile on her face. I never knew I could be pretty, and it seems I'm no longer a girl at all. I look like a young woman from the magazines I've seen in Lost Town.

I pause at the door at the end of the hallway and take a deep breath before knocking. Wudak's voice answers from inside, inviting me in. I step into a room that looks more like a library than a dining hall. The walls are lined with books stretching all the way to the ceiling—old, leather-bound volumes in all the colors of the rainbow.

Three Sliman are waiting, sitting at a heavy, worn table that looks like it could be centuries old. Lit candles flicker softly, their glow casting shadows over the polished wood. A vase of fresh flowers sits at the center.

The Sliman rise, bowing their heads. I glance at Wudak, hoping for some encouragement, but his expression is dark and unreadable.

One of the Sliman steps forward, taking my hand in his. "I am Zolkon," he says, leading me to a chair beside his.

He's the first Sliman I've met who *looks* older. Not old the way humans age, but there are some unmistakable, telltale signs. His eyelids droop slightly, his shoulders are somewhat hunched, and the tattoos on his face have faded.

Just how long has he been alive?

The third Sliman introduces himself as Ludik and then immediately asks for my permission to go.

"Of course," I say, totally confused. I have no idea why he'd ask for my permission, or why he was in the room in the first place.

"Finally," Zolkon says with a hoarse voice as he raises his glass of wine. "I can now say that I have met the magic girl."

I notice that he has several gold rings on his fingers. *Alien gifts.* I get straight to the point. "Do you think you can alter the receptor so that it stays undetectable?"

"I will do my best, my girl. And my best is usually enough." He laughs at his own words before gulping down his wine.

"Freya has made tremendous progress with the receptor," Wudak says and it's nice to see he's in my corner.

"We better not make her angry then," Zolkon says, and his laughter follows once again. He turns to me. "Tell me, Freya, would you be willing to lead a dark legion of the best Sliman warriors? Would you fight with us against the Lagerians and their tyranny?"

"I would do anything that needs to be done to free Earth," I say, cautiously. "Anything that's within my power."

"Don't worry about that; it is well within your power," he says with an enigmatic smile on his face. "All right, let's get started."

He takes the lid off the plate in front of him and reveals a roast with golden potatoes and apples. *Biscuit would have given anything for the recipe,* I think as I taste the succulent, tender meal.

"You haven't tried your wine yet," Zolkon says.

"I've never had wine before," I say and that causes a new bout of laughter from Zolkon.

"Never had wine? My dear girl, how do you deal with this world then? Go ahead, have a sip."

I look at Wudak. He nods, but I can tell he's very unhappy about something. I give it a try. I take a sip.

"Well?" Zolkon asks.

"It's sour and sweet. Not bad at all," I say as I take a second sip. "When are you going to adjust the receptor?" I cannot forget this is the only reason I'm here, not for dressing up and drinking wine.

"First thing tomorrow morning. Wudak will let you know." Zolkon hesitates for a moment. "Can I see it?"

"Why not? What's the point of hiding it now if you're going to hold it in the morning?"

"No point. No point at all," he reassures me.

I have fastened the receptor around my calf, so I have to reach under the table to get it. When I resurface, I think I catch a look of complicity between Zolkon and Wudak. Maybe I'm just imagining things. In any case, I have to be extra careful.

I let Zolkon admire the receptor while I hold it in my hand.

"Yes," he says. "An OS-1456, just like I thought."

"What does that mean?"

"It's one of the most advanced models ever made. It can create energy out of almost nothing. A speck of dust. A dry leaf. A butterfly's wing. It is a mega-projector, turning wishes into energy commands."

It all goes above my head, but I don't want to sound stupid. "It's the one good thing that came out from all their experiments," I say.

"Yes, yes. Good for us. For them, not so much." Zolkon starts laughing again. Every time it gets more and more irritating.

"Freya should rest," Wudak says.

"Of course, where are my manners? Sleep well, dear girl. I will see you in the morning."

There's something very disturbing about Zolkon that I can't quite put my finger on, something besides the obvious flaws in his personality, and I'm glad to get out of there and back to the solitude of my room.

✦

MY HEAD FEELS HEAVY as if a rock presses against it. I try to turn, but the pain is so intense that it locks me to the pillow. I force my eyelids to open and get an annoying buzz in my ears right before the nausea kicks in. I've never felt worse in my life.

I search for the sensory receptor and find it under the pillow. When I touch it, I have a weird sensation, almost as if I'm being watched. I sit up and spot Wudak sitting in the armchair across from my bed. I let out a cry of shock as it takes me a second to realize it's him.

"What are you doing in my room?" I say, pulling the covers over me.

His eyes are darker than ever when he locks them with mine. "I'm sorry," he says. "This was not my intention. It was not my plan. I didn't have all the facts. But as it is, I have no choice."

"What are you talking about? You're scaring me, Wu-dak."

He gets up, walks to me and extends his hand. "Here," he says, "you can touch me. I won't shy away."

"I don't want to touch you."

"Take my hand, Freya. It's an order."

"I don't take orders from you," I say as I rub the recep-tor in my palm.

He grabs my hand and holds it for a few seconds with his eyes shut as a pained expression takes over his face.

"You're freaking me out," I yell, fighting to pull my hand from his lethal grip.

"There, it's done," he says as he lets go.

"Wudak, what is all this?"

"Don't trust anyone," he whispers. "Not even me. You have to find a way to get out of here."

"What's that supposed to mean?" I ask, but he's already gone.

CHAPTER 19

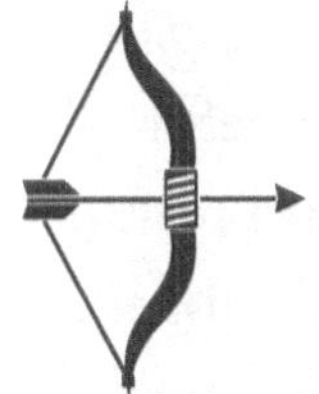

I TRY TO GET out of bed but everything spins. I sit down and close my eyes, trying to recollect my thoughts. Something's wrong with me, that much is obvious. But what? And why?

I look around for my clothes. They're either gone or maybe put in the closet. Who knows who did that or when. Wudak was here, that's true, but he doesn't exactly strike me as someone who would want to clean up.

I drag myself to the closet. I discover a number of dresses, sweaters and fancy shoes, but my own clothes are missing. I'll have to put one of those damned dresses on if I want to get out of this room.

I pick the one that seems to be the least conspicuous. It's a dark blue dress with long sleeves and it goes just above the knee. I choose a pair of blue shoes with three-inch heels. I have no idea how I'm going to be able to walk about in them. I'll demand that my clothes are returned to me, or I will blow the whole place up.

I start taking off my nightgown and then I realize that I don't remember putting it on. The dizziness returns along with an intense feeling of nausea. I barely have time to run to the bathroom before throwing up.

As I clean my face and mouth at the sink, I know beyond the shadow of a doubt that this is not good. I have been misled by Wudak, and Zolkon is not someone to trust. He's not my ally; he has his own agenda. And he made me sick for some reason.

The hallway is dark. The doors and windows are all closed. I fear I have been locked in, but the door to the balcony opens easily and I tiptoe outside. It's the break of dawn and the sky is a beautiful mix of orange and violet. I step inside the circular room with the view to the garden, trying to figure out how to get down there. As I press on the glass with both hands, I feel it give in and take a step back, unsure of what is going on. Then the whole paneling moves out a few feet, revealing a staircase between the glass and the floor.

I go down the stairs and almost slip twice so I take the stupid shoes off and carry them in my left hand. The right hand is clutching onto the sensory receptor. Something doesn't feel right about the receptor, but then again nothing feels right.

The garden is silent, and the fact takes me by complete surprise. The fountain turns out to be an illusion—there's no water flowing, just the projection of water, almost like a mirage. Nothing stirs and nothing makes a peep. There's nothing here but synthetic, rigid vegetation. When I touch the plants, it feels like I'm touching brittle rocks.

Then I hear something. It's ever so slight and I rub my ears hard to make sure they're not playing tricks on me. A few seconds later, I hear the same sound. This time it's a bit louder and I can pinpoint its location. It's coming from the trees in the back.

I drop the shoes and walk toward the direction of the trees.

◆

I SIT IN THE armchair where I found Wudak during the night. The spinning sensation has subsided, and I start to feel like myself again. I won't let Zolkon and Wudak know that I feel better. I will play this out as best as I can. I have to figure out what their plan is before I leave this place. And they can't do anything to stop me. Whatever they have in store for me, I will outsmart them. All those years of living in the wild have not been for nothing. I am resourceful, I am patient. Most of all, I'm in control of my feelings and, therefore, of my receptor.

My receptor. I like the sound of it. For the first time

since I got the sensory receptor device, I don't feel like a misfit. I feel privileged and honored. I am ready.

I wait patiently for Wudak and when he knocks on the door, I let him in with a sigh of pain.

"Good, keep that painful look on for Zolkon," he says. "As for me, I can see right through you."

I'm taken aback by the confidence in his voice. "Fine," I say. "If that's how you want it, that's how we'll play it. Why did you come to my room last night? How long did you stay? Who poisoned me? Who put me in bed? Why?"

"You will soon find out, but I'm not allowed to say anything." He comes closer to me, his face turning dark again. "Your life is in no immediate danger, I can assure you of that. On my honor. On the revolution. Do not fear for your life."

"What should I fear? Is Zolkon hoping to steal the receptor from me? It won't work. Thanks to you, I know what to do."

"Let's go," he says. "Zolkon's waiting." Before we exit, he pauses and whispers, "Remember what I told you last night?"

"Which part?" I say, but I know what he means. I have to find a way to get out of here. And I will. After I'm done with Zolkon.

◈

WE FIND ZOLKON WAITING for us in a semi-dark room that looks suspiciously like a laboratory. Strange, unfamiliar devices clutter tables and shelves alongside familiar lab equipment—microscopes, scanners, and diagnostic monitors. Zolkon is hunched over a worktable, fiddling with a test tube containing a luminous blue fluid. He quickly sets it down and turns, opening his arms in greeting.

"Here you are, dear girl," he says, adjusting his posture. "How was your night?"

"Terrible," I reply. "Something I ate, I guess." I touch my forehead as if my temperature has risen.

"Sit, then, sit," Zolkon says and points at an old desk chair. "We don't want you to get sick, do we?"

I sit on the chair and steal a glance at Wudak. Whatever his thoughts might be, they are impenetrable.

"Did you have anything to eat yet?" Zolkon says.

I shake my head. "I don't think I could hold anything down."

"Let's hope you'll feel better soon. Now, let's begin, shall we? Where's that beautiful OS-1456?"

I show him the receptor, but as he moves in to reach it, I close my fingers around it. "You know what," I say. "I think we shouldn't do this when I feel this lousy. Let's wait until I feel better."

"But of course, of course," he says. "You should rest. You know, I know a few things about medicine and biology. Not too much, the aliens wouldn't trust me with such vital knowledge, but they did show me how to test blood for infections and parasites. Here, see?" He points at an automated microscope. "We'll draw the blood, put it under the lens and we'll know what's wrong with you."

"No, thank you," I say and get up. "Wudak will walk me back."

"Ah, but that won't do, that won't do at all," Zolkon says.

"What do you mean?"

"What I mean is that I need a blood sample from you."

"Well, you can't have it," I say impatiently as I walk away. My nerves are alerted to a danger I cannot quite understand.

"Get her," Zolkon orders.

Wudak doesn't hesitate. He grabs my arm and forces me to sit back on the chair. I will the receptor to turn on, but nothing happens. I try to turn it on manually to no avail.

"In order for it to work, you would need this," Zolkon says as he takes something out of his pocket. It's so small, I can barely see it.

He turns it around in his palm. "Beautiful, don't you think?"

Now I understand. It's a microchip.

"Don't you worry about your indisposition," he goes on. "You've been drugged; it will soon pass." He picks up the test tube with the blue fluid and studies it. "It won't mess with the test. It will all go according to plan."

"What plan?" I yell while Wudak holds me down on the chair.

"Yes, what plan, good question," Zolkon says. "You see, dear child, I need you. There's no other way to put it. If you do as I say, everything will be all right. You will be free to go back to your friends, and you and I will be allies forever. You will be able to count on me."

My mind is reeling. He sounds like the devil himself, only worse because he's real.

He picks up a syringe. "Roll up her sleeve," he orders Wudak.

It's pointless. I can't fight Wudak, not physically, not with my bare hands. So I sit back while he's rolling up my sleeve.

"What happened to the receptor?" I say.

"Let's just say I couldn't trust you with it. I knew you might try to use it on us. Wudak disabled it on my command."

He sinks the needle in my vein and the blood starts flowing inside the syringe. I let him go on with his account of the events as I'm having trouble forming the right words to say.

"I have no interest in the receptor," Zolkon says. "Just you. You are the real weapon in the war. My weapon."

I turn and face Wudak when he lets go of my arm.

"What did you do?"

Zolkon looks at me, amused. "He got you to trust him, didn't he? Beautiful, just beautiful. I should take lessons from him."

I feel a knot in my throat. "What did you have him do?"

"Having you in the lab with the receptor was no option. Something had to be done about it. There was a chance the receptor would react to your nerve impulses even when you were asleep, which is why we gave you the wine. I believe it worked great, don't you think, Wudak? I mean, you don't have any recollection of him taking the receptor from under your pillow and removing its core chip, do you?"

Now it all makes sense. Everything. I have been trapped. I'm as good as dead. The thought of the arrogance, the nerve and stupidity of my actions freezes me.

"How did he do that?" I whisper.

"It's really easy. Do you see that tiny slot on the side of the receptor?"

I turn the receptor around.

"Right there," Zolkon says.

I see it. It's the tiniest slot. I don't know why I never noticed it before.

"That's where the chip goes," Zolkon says. "It fits in seamlessly."

I guess that's why.

"Once you know how to retrieve it, it's a matter of seconds."

"And the receptor is useless without it," I murmur.

"Oh, yes, quite useless. It's like a human without a nervous system. Or a Sliman. Anything really. No nervous system, no functionality. You may return to your room now. I'll see you again tomorrow when I return from the plantation. And don't even think about escaping. The fortress is guarded on the outside and the inside. I wouldn't want you to get hurt."

"No," I say. "I won't go until you tell me why you need me. Are you going to negotiate with the aliens over me?"

"No, no, far from it. You, my dear, will help me get the Sliman from under the Lagerian grip. In return, you and your little friends will be spared and will be able to live however you want."

"How are you going to use me?" I insist.

"All in good time. You will know soon enough. Wudak, take her back."

❖

"Is that what you were sorry for?" I ask Wudak right before he leaves me alone in the room.

"That and more," he says.

"I suppose you're not going to tell me what *and more* refers to."

He shakes his head.

"Yeah, I didn't think so."

"You have every right to be angry with me," he says.

"You think so? I should have known better than to trust a single word that came out of a Sliman's mouth."

"I will protect you. That hasn't changed."

"Oh, yeah, and I should believe that because your word is as good as gold." I sit down and look at the receptor. "It's a useless toy now. All this effort for nothing. Why didn't you just take the whole thing?"

"So that you wouldn't be alarmed. Remember what I said," he says, but he doesn't look at me.

"What, you want me to escape? How do you propose I do that? Are you going with me? Will you fight all your Slimie friends around the spooky castle?"

"I can't do that. I'm not going to lie to you anymore."

"Too little, too late."

"You'll figure it out," he says. He goes through my backpack and takes my pulse gun.

"That's just great," I say as he leaves.

I wait until it gets dark, and I sneak out of the room and into the garden. I head straight for the fake plastic trees, or whatever it is they're made of. This is my only option and my only hope.

CHAPTER 20

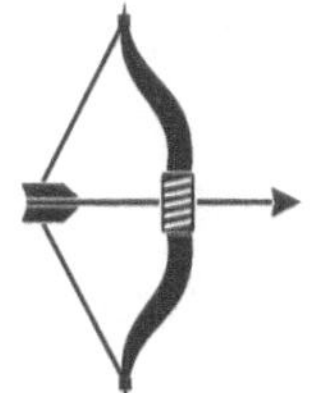

I WAKE UP STARTLED by the sound of loud footsteps marching around the fortress. Then the voices follow. My captors have discovered I didn't spend the night in my room. I get up slowly and move away from the trees. My knees feel sore and my neck hurts, but it's nothing compared to what I felt when I woke up yesterday.

I lie down on a bench in a clear spot of the garden where I can be seen easily. Two Sliman spot me from the windows above and come running down the stairs. They're about to grab me but suddenly stop cold in their tracks and look at each other instead. It's curious how Sliman are never willing to touch me, grab me, shoot me or stab me. It's almost as if they know I'm a weapon, as Zolkon put it, whatever that may mean.

Wudak shows up just in time. "What are you doing here? Zolkon—"

"What? Did he get upset? Did he think I vanished out of thin air?"

"You don't want to make him angry, Freya."

"Don't ever call me by my name, do you hear me? There's no friendship between us, no understanding, no alliance, no nothing."

He grabs my arm and all but drags me all the way to my room. He, at least, has definitely overcome his fear of my touch. When we get there, he notices I'm barefoot and my feet have been badly scraped from the friction as he pulled me across the castle's stone pathways and wooden floors.

"What am I going to do with you?" he murmurs, almost as if talking to himself. He disappears into the bathroom and returns moments later with a bowl of warm water and some clean bandages. Without a word, he places them in front of me.

I dip a cloth into the warm water, carefully wiping away the dirt and blood from my skin. The cuts sting at the contact, but I keep going. Once done, I wrap the fresh bandages around my feet.

"You can go now," I say.

"If it were up to me, I'd find a different way to do this."

"Is this supposed to make me feel better?"

"Maybe it would be better if we stopped talking to each other," he says after a brief pause.

I don't have time to respond. The door opens and the great Zolkon himself marches in.

"Well, well, what do we have here?" he says. He takes one glance at me and frowns. "My dear girl, look at you, you're a mess. Get cleaned up, put a nice dress on and come to the lab. Or would you rather have an escort?"

"No," I say. "I can manage on my own just fine."

"Good, good. I'll see you in an hour then." The room fills up with his hideous laughter, making the core of my being crawl with disgust.

My knees shake slightly as I brace myself to enter Zolkon's lab of horrors. I don't know what he has in store, but I can't let him think I'm scared.

"Ah, so much better," he says when I walk in. "That's how I envision a queen, dressed in radiating white and wearing a confident smile. Sit, sit."

He points at that old chair again. I sit down and straighten the dress on my thighs. It was a pain to put on and a pain to sit in. It's really tight around the waist and thighs and leaves my back naked. I feel like I've been stuck inside a hose.

"Since I'm obviously at your mercy," I start, "where's the harm in telling me what you plan to do with me? What is it that makes me such a special weapon in your fight for independence?"

"Fair enough," he says. "It's not an unreasonable request. Let me check that test tube first." As he says this, he opens what seems to be a small freezer and takes out a tube that contains something brownish.

"My blood, I guess," I say.

"Yes, yes, but so much more than that also. It's been mixed with a binder that will let us test it for compatibility. So that we are absolutely certain."

"Compatibility with what?" I ask, alarmed.

"The embryo of course," he says, laughing.

Something drops in my stomach. "What embryo?" I ask, shellshocked.

"Wudak told you that you're an alien host," he says as he opens the tube and lets a drop of brown blood land under the lens of the microscope.

"He also told me that's the reason you don't want aliens to get to me," I say, trembling now.

"Oh, yes, it's true, I'd never let the aliens capture you." The smile disappears from his face. "I'd rather have you killed first," he says, coldly. Then, almost immediately, the smile returns. "We don't have to worry about that though. The aliens don't know about any of this."

He closes one eye and uses the other to examine the sample under the microscope. Then he picks up the test tube and empties its content in a different glass tube that's connected to some type of small data processor.

"This is the compatibility analyzer," he announces. "It will let us know soon enough."

"If you can do that, how come you can't reproduce Omicron 5?"

"Omicron 5!" he exclaims with an amused expression. "You know a lot more than I thought. However, dearest child, this is pretty much the only thing I can do. Analyze blood samples, I mean. I've prepared for this moment for a long time. Everything you see here I had to steal from discard bins at the plantation labs. Omicron 5 is just about the most complicated formula ever invented in the known universe. It would require knowledge and technology that is far beyond me or any Sliman."

"I still don't know what you're planning to do with me."

"Okay, here it is. You are going to give me an alien baby. Then I will let you go. I will raise that baby until he's old enough to use the Lagerian sensory technology. Then... well, you needn't worry about the rest."

"You stole an embryo?" I say, still in disbelief.

"Yes, I did. Their time will be up soon."

"And you will be ruler of the world."

"I never said that, did I?"

"You don't have to."

"You're a smart girl. Maybe too smart. But none of it matters. You just relax."

Wudak comes in and hands Zolkon a touchpad. Zolkon takes it and reads something on the screen. "Very well," he says with a smile. "Everything's going according to plan." He turns to me. "Now don't you worry about a thing. It won't hurt a bit. Just one more needle and that's it."

I feel like screaming, but I have to stay focused. I know my options. None of them are easy, but I will do what I have to do.

The compatibility analyzer beeps and Zolkon rubs his hands together. "That's it then," he says. "The moment of truth."

I avoid looking at Wudak. What I feel for him right now resembles hatred and I can't afford to have such strong feelings. He is meaningless to me. That's what I need to focus on.

Zolkon removes a small glass screen from the analyzer and observes the graphs on it. The more he studies them, the more his expression turns to that of fury and anger. He drops the screen and attacks Wudak out of the blue. He punches him hard on the face twice and then uses his knee to kick him in the stomach. "What have you done, you idiot?" he shouts.

Wudak is taken aback and doesn't react at first. When Zolkon attempts to punch him again, he finally comes to his senses and pushes Zolkon away.

"What are you doing?" he yells.

"What do you think?" Zolkon yells back. He picks up the glass screen and hands it to Wudak. "Read!" he orders him.

"That's impossible," Wudak says after looking at what-ever is on that screen. He glances at me, then back at the screen in his hand. "I have no idea how this could have happened," he tells Zolkon. "It's obviously a mistake, run it again."

"Take her to her room," Zolkon fumes. "And keep her chained!"

◆

"What happened back there?" I ask Wudak as he puts a handcuff around my wrist.

"Nothing that should be any concern of yours," he says. He puts the second handcuff around the bed pole and locks it.

"I hope it's not too uncomfortable," he says.

"You know he wants to run the world, right?"

"Don't you have enough problems of your own right now?"

"I wouldn't know, nobody tells me anything," I say, batting my lashes as innocently as possible.

"Listen here, I just bought you a little bit of time. It won't last. Figure something out. And stop looking so pleased with yourself. Unless you know something that I don't."

I shrug. He looks at me for a moment and then he goes. Yes, there are things that he doesn't know. He doesn't know that I have a chimp named Shy Boy. He doesn't know that my chimp would follow me to the end of the world. He doesn't know that he found a way to climb inside the fortress. He doesn't know that I found him hiding in the garden last night. And he definitely doesn't know that Shy Boy is on his way to the underground camp and that he won't rest until he hands Finn my touchpad with the message I put there for him.

❖

TIME GOES BY SLOWLY like a feather falling to the ground from considerable height. Change is what makes time bearable. Moving from the table to the bed, from inside outside, from unhappy to happy, from sick to healthy. I'm trapped in a sticky sameness in here. For how many hours I don't know.

The Sliman guard named Ludik came in once and brought me water, bread and fruit. I gulped everything down. I need to stay strong. How many hours is it since Shy Boy left? Will he manage to get back to the base and get Finn's attention somehow? Will they come for me in time? Yes, they will. I have to believe that.

Ludik comes back with more food and water. It's getting dark outside. How does desolation look when the sky goes black?

"What time is it?" I ask Ludik but get no response.

MY EYES ARE HEAVY. Maybe I should try and get some sleep. I need to be strong, and I can't be strong if I don't sleep. I close my eyes for a few seconds and watch the moving shadows and images that form underneath my eyelids as if they were a movie. Then I hear his voice. It comes like a whisper, an airy wave of hope. "Freya."

I open my eyes in an instant. "Over here."

He comes to me. His hands search for me and when he finds me, he hugs me and holds my face close to his chest. His arms feel so powerful, so comforting and healing that I let a sob out. He kisses my hair and my face, and we are both unable to say a single thing.

My eyes adjust better to the darkness, and I make out the shape of his face. His face that I didn't know I'd come to cherish like this. I reach over with my free hand to turn on the lamp on the night table. I find the shock in his eyes amusing when he sees the white dress and the hairdo.

"Wow, you look... different," he says, but then he notices the handcuffs. "What have they done to you?"

"Nothing yet." My words don't appease him. He growls like a savage, angry that I'm handcuffed to a bed like a prisoner. "Damian, we have to get out of here fast. How did you get inside the fortress without being noticed?"

"Your chimp found an opening high up on the wall behind the garden. Finn and I helped each other climb it."

"Finn's here, too?"

"Yes, we split up, so we could search faster. There are no guards in the fortress, no cameras, nothing. So at first I thought your chimp brought us to the wrong place." He takes his pulse gun out and recalibrates the settings. He plans to use it on the handcuff lock.

"No," I say, "don't do that. Let Finn find me."

I can tell that he thinks I'm joking. "What are you talking about? Have you lost your mind?"

"You can't save my life twice, it's not fair to Finn," I insist. "It's bad enough that I will have to tell him about you and me."

He considers this for a moment and then shakes his head. "You're crazy. Look where you are. The Sliman could come back at any moment."

I push his hand away from the handcuff. "I know, but this is what I want."

"Fine, have it your way. But this is the last time I will take second place to Finn. I'll direct him here somehow."

I wrap my free hand around his neck and kiss him. It feels so good that I fear I won't be able to let him go. It feels like home if ever I had one.

He takes a deep breath in when our lips part before he rests his forehead against mine.

"Were you serious? You'll tell Finn about us?"

"Of course. What did you think? That I would lie to him?"

"I thought maybe you changed your mind."

"I didn't. Now go."

I know that he doesn't want to leave me, but he grants my wish. I bring my fingers to my lips to feel his warmth again. I hear my heartbeat in my ears and I don't know how to calm it down.

When Finn shows up minutes later, his hair is all messed up. "Tick," he says, staring at me dumbfounded. That stupid dress again no doubt. "It's really you," he says finally.

"Of course, it's me. Did Shy Boy find you?"

"He did. He practically stormed into the base. He brought us all back here. Pip is very worried, you know."

"Pip is here?"

"Yes, everyone is. We couldn't leave them at the Sliman base after your message. They're hiding behind the boulders beyond the gates. Wudak betrayed all of us, not just you."

He frees my hand by cutting a hole through the lock of the handcuff with a laser beam from his pulse gun. He helps me up to my feet.

"Here, put this in your backpack," I say as I throw the receptor at him. "Now let's go find Damian."

Finn pauses. "How do you know he's inside the fortress?"

"You said so."

"No, I didn't."

"As if he'd just let you come in alone and be the hero. Let's go."

He doesn't question this any further. We get out of the room and go down the hallway. We bump into Damian right as we step onto the balcony.

"This way," I say and lead them to the circular room with the panel windows. I press my hand on the glass until it gives way and then we dash down the stairs. There's a full moon tonight making the garden look hauntingly beautiful.

"Wait!" I say. This is ridiculous, I can't run in this dress. I pull the fabric apart all the way up to my thighs. "That's better."

We run down the stairs again. The opening on the wall must be right behind the plastic trees.

I get a jolt of fright down my spine when Zolkon steps out of the trees, holding a gun, with Ludik close behind him.

"Dear girl," he says with a big smile. "Where do you think you're going?" Then the smile fades, and he locks his gaze on Damian as if he just saw a ghost.

"It was you," he says, slowly. "That certainly explains, well... almost everything."

Damian reaches for his gun, quietly staring back into Zolkon's eyes.

"Now, don't do that," Zolkon says, his eyes fixed on Damian's hand. "I really don't want to kill you, but luckily I have another option." He raises his gun and points it at Finn's head. Ludik draws his gun and turns it on Damian almost simultaneously.

"No," I yell and jump in front of Finn. "Drop the gun, Damian."

Damian returns the gun to its holster. Zolkon laughs with that hideous laughter of his that makes me want to break every tooth in his mouth. "You can't save them both no matter what you do, silly girl," he says. "Maybe I'll make you pick one."

"That's enough, Zolkon," Wudak says as he walks down the staircase.

"I will say when it's enough," Zolkon says, irritated.

Wudak turns to Damian. "Get Freya out of here."

"Did you know about him?" Zolkon asks with his gun still pointed at Finn.

"Yes," Wudak says as he steps in front of me.

"What is it that you knew? What is he saying about Damian?" I ask.

Wudak shakes his head. "Not now, Freya. Just go."

Zolkon's eyes focus on Wudak curiously. "Why didn't you tell me? It was your duty. You are a soldier."

"Precisely for this reason," Wudak says, pointing at

Zolkon's raised gun.

"Get out of the way, Wudak, or I will raise the alarm."

"You could, except I've sent all the guards back to their plantations."

"You would defy me and our hierarchy in order to protect a human girl? Do you know the punishment for that?" Zolkon bellows.

"I know everything that I need to know," Wudak responds. "Now lower your gun."

"Anybody move half a muscle and the boy dies," Zolkon says, taking a step toward Finn.

"Have it your way," Wudak says. Within the blink of an eye, he jumps on Zolkon and Ludik, throwing them both to the ground just with the sheer force and weight of his body. Two pulse guns go off and, in the confusion, Damian pulls his gun and shoots Ludik as he tries to get up.

Wudak holds Zolkon down, covering him with his entire body. Then Zolkon manages to push Wudak off him. As Wudak rolls on his back, I notice a red stain on his abdomen.

Finn and Damian both hold their pulse guns against Zolkon.

"You fool," Zolkon yells at Wudak. "What did you do? Did you let her touch you? Did you bond with her?"

"Don't shoot him," I tell Finn and Damian. "We need answers from him. He has the core of the receptor." I drop to my knees next to Wudak. He's bleeding bad, but he's still breathing. "Why did you do that?"

Wudak opens his mouth, and a pink foam oozes out.

"No, don't talk," I say. "Doc is here, he will fix you. Call him, Damian."

"Communications don't work in this district," Damian says.

"Go get him then. Get everyone."

"What's the point? Let's kill them both and get the hell out of here."

"Wudak saved us," I say, raising my voice. "Use your brain, Damian, we're nothing without the receptor. We might as well surrender. We need them both alive."

Damian curses under his breath as he goes to get Doc and the others. Finn takes a second pulse gun out of his backpack and throws it at me. I catch it in midair, and then I look at Zolkon. "Tell me what you meant about Damian. What is it about him that got you so interested?"

"I don't think I'll tell you anything," Zolkon says. "At this point, you need me more than I need you."

"I won't kill you, but I will maim you," I say and point the gun at his foot.

"Tough. I like tough. Tell me, do you see that little transmitter on the ground?" Zolkon says. I look down and spot a small device much like a touchpad. "A few minutes ago, I pushed button number 3. Do you know what this means?"

Wudak groans. "Freya," he whispers. "Danger."

"Shush," I say. "Don't exert yourself."

"What he's trying to tell you is that pretty soon the whole place will be swarming with Sliman and Lagerians," Zolkon says. "You have maybe three minutes. How tough are you now?"

"You're bluffing."

"Freya," Wudak calls my name again. "He gave... your... position... with number 3."

The pink foam flows freely out of his mouth again, and I tear a piece of my dress to clean his face. I glance at Finn. My heart sinks. He doesn't think this is a bluff.

"You transmitted a message to the aliens?" I ask Zolkon. "Why? You said they were your enemies. You want to bring them down."

"Well, I can't do that anymore. Not with you out of the picture. If you can't beat them, join them. That's the name of the game."

Finn knocks him on the head with his gun and Zolkon loses his balance and falls.

"He's telling the truth, isn't he?" Finn says.

My response is drowned out by a deafening sound.

Zolkon laughs as loud as he can. "The drone!" he yells.

CHAPTER 21

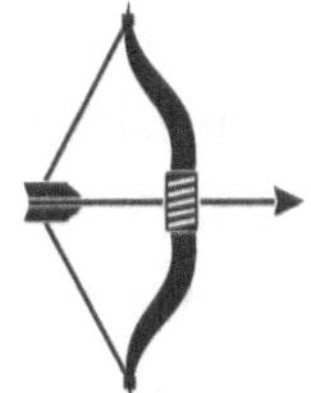

THE DRONE LIGHTS UP the sky and earth with its search beams, sweeping over the fortress walls. The noise subsides once it locks into position, hovering only yards away. It looks like a huge helicopter without windows, made of some kind of dense metal that seems impenetrable.

Finn yanks me down, wrapping his arms around me as we drop to the ground. We stare at the sky in awe. Zolkon has disappeared. The underside of the drone splits open, releasing a mob of Sliman who climb down rope ladders. The gunfire begins instantly. Outside the fortress, the Saviors are under attack.

I push up on my elbows. "We have to help."

Finn's grip tightens. "It's you they want, Freya." The overwhelming sadness on his face is something I didn't expect to see again.

"And they'll kill everyone to get to me if they have to.

I can't let that happen, Finn."

"Are you going to give yourself up again? It didn't work last time."

"Who knows, maybe an idiot will throw a second receptor at me," I say jokingly, but it's all bittersweet now.

I push myself up and glance back at Wudak lying on the ground. I raise my hand in farewell, but he grabs my ankle.

"Freya, let's go," Finn urges me, growing frantic as the shooting intensifies.

"He's trying to tell us something."

I drop to my knees, pressing my ear close to Wudak's mouth. His breath is shallow, his body trembling with the effort to speak. He struggles to lift his hand, and I reach out, clasping it in mine. I feel something cold in his palm.

The missing chip.

Wudak tries to smile, but pink foam bubbles at his lips. "He's not so smart," he whispers hoarsely. His body shudders with a cough. "I took this when I jumped on him."

My eyes well up. There's nothing I can do to stop the tears. I can't take any more losses, any more death. I can't take one more moment of pointless, meaningless suffering. I press a kiss to Wudak's forehead. "I'll come back for you," I whisper.

Wudak's fingers go slack.

"Freya," Finn calls. "Are you okay?"

"Oh, yeah. I'm better than okay," I say, wiping away the

tears. "Hand me that receptor. I have the missing piece." I rise to my feet, holding up the chip. "Now let's go fry some Sliman."

The bandages slip from my feet as we sprint to the front gates. The drone above immediately turns its ugly nose on us.

I grin up at it. "Damn right, I'm here." I turn to Finn. "Stay close to me. They won't blow me up just yet."

I raise the sensory receptor and direct it toward the battlefield. The Saviors have barricaded themselves behind a jagged line of rocks about my height, using them as cover while they're fighting a horde of Sliman warriors. There's forty, maybe fifty of them, enraged and relentless, but they can't get close to the rocks. Damian and Nya lead the charge, taking a lot of risk every time they climb onto the rocks to fire at the advancing Sliman.

They don't hesitate. They can't. I won't hesitate either.

I channel my energy into the receptor, creating a shield around the barricade—an invisible force field that will deflect laser blasts and magnetic knives, sending them bouncing away. The moment the Sliman realize what I'm doing, their heads snap up, searching for me and the receptor.

"Oh, yes, come to me."

A surge of raw energy pulses through my body. I extend my arm and unleash a massive electric wave, fast as lightning, precise as a blade. It slams into the main body of the Sliman unit. Screams tear through the battlefield as they crumble, writhing in pain. Above us, the drone shifts slightly, its massive form adjusting as if reevaluating the situation.

Good. Let them rethink their choices.

But I don't take a single moment to rest. The risk doesn't matter. The exhaustion that will inevitably follow doesn't matter. I have to strike while they're still confused. I close my eyes, focusing every ounce of my internal energy into the receptor. When I squeeze it tighter, a phosphorescent green light explodes outward, stretching across the battlefield, attacking everything in sight—everything outside of the blue shield protecting the Saviors.

I have created two different fields: one that protects and one that destroys. *Cool.*

The Sliman who escaped the electric blast, freeze in place, their bodies turning stiff and lifeless within seconds of being touched by the green light.

I quickly scan the battlefield, assessing the situation. I don't see a single Sliman who could still put up a fight. I obliterated their whole damned battalion in two strikes. That's what my rage can do now. Someday, I'll be able to do it all at will.

My gaze snaps upward. The drone looms overhead. Can I reach it? If I unleash the full power of the receptor, could I take it down?

And what would that do to me? Or anyone else on the ground?

Finn's hand lands on my shoulder. I jerk in surprise, so lost in thoughts of the battle I forgot he was even there.

He doesn't have to say a word. I *know* he's read my mind. He knows I want to take aim at the drone. I can feel it in his troubled gaze, his protective hand.

"Hold on to me," I shout. "Don't let go! It's going to be bumpy."

Finn grips my arm just as I close my eyes again. I don't know why the drone hasn't released its wrath on us yet. I don't know why it just hovers above our heads, watching, but I won't wait to find out. Maybe the aliens didn't expect to find me holding a working receptor.

I don't know if I'm strong enough, but I need to be, and that's all that counts. When I open my eyes, the ground starts trembling. A purple energy whirlwind forms in front of my eyes. At first, it's so small it can fit in my palm, but it grows, expanding, twisting, spiraling out of control until it becomes gigantic, reaching skyward to encircle the drone like a furious storm, shaking it with incredible violence.

Out of the corner of my eye, I see Damian scrambling onto the rocks.

"Stay down," I shout, but he doesn't hear me. He probably wouldn't stay down even if he did. "Keep everyone safe," I whisper as I'm getting ready to deliver the blow that will bring the drone down.

I know my hand won't be able to handle the ferocity of my attempt even before a piercing pain shoots through my shoulder blades, neck and arms. Every nerve in my body screams. The feeling is so unbearable that I clench my teeth, tightening every muscle to keep from collapsing. My knees buckle, but Finn is already there, holding me up, keeping me from hitting the ground.

Then the underside of the drone opens again, and a searing blue beam slices through my whirlwind, traveling fast toward Finn and me. It takes all I have to stop it from striking us, but I won't be able to hold it back for long.

The energy crackles and pulses against my resistance. My body feels like it's splitting apart, the pain now radiating through my spine, my knees, even my feet and toes. My ears ring with the shrillest of sounds. I get lightheaded. I can barely make out Damian and the others as they rush toward Finn and me.

Rabbit outruns everyone and gets to me first. He holds on to me, trying to offer me extra support. But it's not physical support that I need. I need internal strength; I need to find a second source of energy within me, and I don't know how to do that.

I think of my mother's hands bathing me as a little girl. Her touch is warm and soft. I hear my big brother's voice talking about distant stars, places he'll never see. I scream as loud as I can. A raw, primal cry, tearing from the depths of me. The surge of energy obliterates the blue beam, then slams into the drone, blowing it up into thousands of burning pieces.

The blast knocks me off my feet, depleted of strength. I manage, somehow, to summon enough power to throw up a shield around us like a protective dome that deflects the sudden tornado of twisted metal raining down on us. Everyone hits the ground, bracing for impact as jagged shards crash down like shrapnel.

Sparks fly as the shards ricochet off the curved surface of my shield. The force of it all rattles through me, draining every last ounce of my will. The final pieces of wreckage strike, sliding down harmlessly.

I slip away. The shield vanishes.

My mother's hands in the bath water. The sun through the window.

"Wake up," I hear Damian's voice.

"Freya, open your eyes," Pip begs of me.

I blindly reach out for the receptor. Someone places it in my hand. *I need you*, I whisper to it. *I need your energy. Fix me.*

Then I feel the jolt. A different kind of jolt, an invigorating stream of warm fluids running through my spine and arteries. The physical warmth and strength are accompanied by an exhilaration of emotions. I don't know what these sensations are. I have nothing to compare them to.

I spring to my feet with renewed energy. I have no idea how long it will last, but I'm not about to waste any time. I get ready to attack the drone again but then I remember—I destroyed it already. Around me, Rabbit, Biscuit, Tilly, Pip, Scout, and even Nya stand up and start cheering. It all feels surreal, making me dizzy.

Our joy is short-lived when a second drone appears in the sky, closing in fast. At the same time, Zolkon emerges from the chaos with an entire legion of bloodthirsty Sliman warriors at his back. I've never seen Sliman that looked bigger or more lethal. They must be a new breed. I remember Zolkon's words. *The Dark Legion.*

I attack them with an electric field, but most of them evade it, moving with terrifying speed. They are not just faster—they're more agile, stronger, smarter than any Sliman I've fought before. They don't fire at my shield. *They know.* They've been trained for this. For me. For the receptor. They were designed to counter everything I am.

Never mind that. The real problem is the new drone hovering above our heads. When the rope ladders drop, I know we'll be surrounded by more Sliman in no time.

"I'm dropping the shield," I yell. "Get ready! I'm going to attack."

We form a tight circle, so our backs are protected. Then I let go. The instant the shield drops, I release a green energy field that sweeps the Sliman off the ground, hurling them hundreds of feet up in the air before gravity forces them back down. I reform the shield, choose a new target, and drop it again.

Another blast. More Sliman wiped out.

Again.

And again.

I'm blasting them left and right. Some stagger back up for a second round, but their numbers are thinning. We work as one, like a synchronized machine of destruction. When I lift the shield, the Saviors go on the attack, and I unleash hell.

The battle is exhausting, but the Sliman forces are nearly defeated. Zolkon is watching from a distance with a grin on his face. I don't understand what he's so happy about until Rabbit crumples to the ground with a hole the size of a quarter burned through his left shoulder blade. A smaller one sears his upper chest.

Laser fire from the drone.

A relentless assault is released from above, as laser beams tear through the battlefield. I throw the shield up just in time, deflecting the onslaught. Doc rushes to Rabbit's side, but I barely register what happens. The realization slams into me.

We're trapped.

More Sliman emerge from the horizon, arriving in heavily armored vehicles. If I attack the drone, I'll have to drop the shield. And the moment I do, the Sliman will swarm us.

"Take the drone out," Damian commands. His eyes are wild. "I'll handle the Sliman." He turns to Nya. "Get your explosive arrows in order, we have work to do."

Nya quickly draws her last three explosive arrows from their sheath. They're all she has left. Maybe all she'll ever have.

I decide to trust Damian. I lift the shield and target the drone with a violent whirlwind, hoping to rip through its defenses.

Nya takes aim, then releases her first arrow, and a blast erupts among the advancing Sliman. The force of it shakes the ground. Damian and Finn cover her as she reloads. They shift, giving her a clear shot, and she launches the second arrow.

My whirlwind grinds against the drone's blue beam as I glance to my right to watch Nya's arrow arc down and deliver its payload of vengeance. The explosion rips through the battlefield, shredding anything in its path.

The few surviving Sliman start to retreat, but Nya's final arrow chases after them and wipes them out. I try not to think about Rabbit. If I do that, I'll break and everything will be lost.

I feel the drone submitting to my will, like a leaf in the wind. I can blow it away with a simple flick of my wrist—and I would do just that except my focus is divided by the arrival of another drone.

I don't know if I have the strength to face it.

I hear Zolkon shout behind me, "They are both here! Position 1-8-4."

I whip around to see him barking coordinates into a touchpad—right before a magnetic hook drops toward me from the drone above. I react only because the receptor wants me to react. It practically forces my hand, pushing an energy blast that strikes the hook before it can latch onto me. I point the receptor at the drone when I suddenly feel something slam into my left calf like a sharp rock.

Zolkon shot me!

It all happens very fast now. I hit the ground. The receptor slips from my grip. Dozens of magnetic hooks descend from the sky amongst a shower of laser beams. They pulse with energy as if they were alive. Finn launches himself at the ropes holding the hooks, hacking through them with rapid strikes, while the other Saviors scatter to avoid getting pierced or shot.

Pip drops down beside me, and I throw my arms around her, shielding her body with my own.

Rabbit is still unconscious. Doc and Theo grab him, dragging him behind a rock for cover.

A penetrating rage consumes me as Zolkon picks up the receptor and turns to face me, his fingers curling possessively around the device.

A sneer twists his face. "I'm sorry it had to come to this, my dear girl, but if I have to choose between you and me, well, you lose every time."

He yanks Pip by the hair, tearing her away from me. I try to lunge forward, but my leg refuses to cooperate. Another Sliman grabs Pip as Zolkon searches for the tiny slot that holds the receptor's core chip. He finds it within seconds. His hideous laugh assaults my ears—the next moment he is shot in the shoulder from above. He staggers back, howling in pain.

I look up, savoring the irony. "Looks like the aliens have no more use for you," I say. I stretch out my hand, calling to the receptor. It jumps back to my hand eagerly. It knows to reboot my body's energy. I feel the refreshing jolt through my veins, the power snapping into place, and I wield it like it's all mine. The Sliman warrior releases Pip and raises his hands in surrender. I let him run away.

As I attack the first of the two drones, I turn the energy field into a heat wave, directing it at the fuel deposit. It ignites, setting the hull on fire. The drone lingers for a breath, burning, before exploding into the sky. I create a magnetic field around Finn, Pip and me to shield us from the blast wave. The other Saviors are at a safe distance, forming a ground perimeter.

Sweat drips down into my eyes as my breathing turns quick and shallow. I will not give out. Not yet. I have to finish this. I lock onto the last drone as it starts to retreat. My final trick is something I feel rather than know, something I've never trained for or even heard Wudak mention. I send a deep purple field into the sky. It expands into a web of energy and grabs the drone, stopping its flight. It thrashes against my hold, but I don't let go, concentrating on a single idea: I want to slam the drone against the fortress to smash it like a bug.

Then I hear him scream.

Damian.

The drone has him. Two hooks have pierced through his arms, lifting him off the ground. His body dangles, writhing in agony as the drone pulls him higher. My heart stops. How did I lose focus? My rage blinded me. Wudak warned me of this.

"No," I yell as I release the drone. It would kill him to destroy it. Damian is too high to cut himself free. He is too far away for me to catch up with. But I run after him. I run like I can chase down the sky. I'm a puny human. I cannot catch them. I run anyway until the drone is a speck on the horizon.

I hear footsteps behind me. I turn and collapse into Finn's arms.

"We have to get him," I choke out through sobs. "We have to run, Finn."

"He's gone, Freya," he whispers.

"No!" I slap him all over his face and chest, anywhere I can reach, again and again.

Finn takes every blow. Then he grabs my shoulders, shaking me hard. "You have to accept it. He's gone. He's as good as dead. Even if they don't kill him, even if they keep him alive, he'll never be the same."

He kisses my forehead, and I push him away. "Rabbit needs you," he says, hurt. "You're his only hope."

I don't know how to say this to him. I'm empty, I don't know how to help anyone. He lifts me up and carries me back to the others. My tears are hot and salty. Everything hurts now. My hands, my arms, my legs, my heart. Everything that I am screams in agony.

Finn sets me down, grips my hand and pulls me forward. I am useless. The sunrise greets the world with a deathly desert orange. Every face is different now. The Saviors are stained with a filthy truth about a filthy lie, the lie that we could win without any sacrifices.

I drop to my knees beside Rabbit. Then I notice something else. A few feet away another body lies on the ground. The body of a Sliman. *Wudak.*

"How did he get here?" I ask.

Zoe hugs me. Her eyes are hollow with a pain almost as deep as mine. She points at a dark figure several yards away. "Gritu found him and brought him here. Wudak said the receptor has healing powers. You have to feel it in you, Freya. You have to save Rabbit."

"I want to," I say as my voice breaks. "I don't know how."

Zoe grips my shoulders, her fingers digging in. "You almost did it for Daphne. I know you can do it now."

"There's nothing I can do for him anymore, Freya," Doc says in anguish.

"Please, Freya," Scout pleads through her tears.

"I will try," I say, "but I'm just a human girl."

Wudak's hand reaches out to me. "It's deep within, find it."

I nod. "First Rabbit and then you."

"The first one... will almost kill you," he whispers. "Just the boy."

I have to pull myself together. I touch Rabbit's forehead. He's burning up. I close my eyes and concentrate on the receptor in my tight fist. Nothing happens. I try again, but I can't get the device to respond.

Then I remember Wudak's words. *You will become the receptor, and it will become you. Its heart beats within you. You are bonded.*

Bonded. That word. Zolkon said that Wudak had bonded with me when he touched me. The receptor has bonded with me. All three can be one.

"Guide me, Wudak. Guide me while you yet breathe."

Wudak smiles up to me. "Take anything you want," he whispers.

I close my eyes and *think* it. *Take anything you want.*

A rainbow of light jumps out of my fingers, the burst of energy so bright my friends stagger back in awe. It's the same rainbow that helped Daphne open her eyes. Is it enough to keep Rabbit among the living?

The flood of light grows wider and brighter, consuming everything in sight. I can barely see anything through it. I turn it on Rabbit and the rays narrow on him, lighting up his face. The light spills down onto his shoulder and across his chest where the deep wounds are killing him. Now a pulse of yellow light sparks out of the receptor and rushes into the wounds. Rabbit convulses as the light flows into him forcefully.

I fight to hold the energy as steady as I can, but a void gradually grows inside me, numbing entire areas of my body, devouring my strength. Rabbit opens his eyes with a jolt. I have to keep him here. I'll bring him back even if it costs me my life.

His wounds start to heal right in front of our stunned eyes. First the bleeding stops, then the torn flesh knits itself together and scabs over.

When the skin starts to heal around the wounds, I pass out.

CHAPTER 22

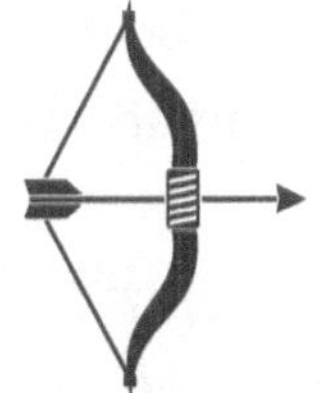

WHEN I COME TO, Rabbit is bending over me. "Welcome back," he says.

"Rabbit, are we alive?" I mutter.

"We are. You saved me, Freya. Thank you."

I try to sit up, but the vertigo pushes me right back.

"Stay still," Doc says. "I don't want to scare you, but your heart stopped. For a moment, you were gone. I wasn't sure we'd get you back. I need you to take it easy."

I realize we're in the fortress and I'm lying on a bed but not the one that was supposed to be mine. I haven't seen this room before. "How long have I been out?"

"A few hours," Doc says. "I took care of your calf wound as best I could. I found medical supplies in here."

"Where's Pip? Finn?"

"They're right outside, I'll get them for you."

"Rabbit," I say, "I'm so glad you're okay. I wanted to see you run again."

Finn and Pip step in the room and Pip runs straight to me. I realize how bad it must be when even Pip knows not to hug me. I cannot even raise my hand to touch her.

Finn kisses my forehead softly. "Don't ever do that again."

"Finn, why are we still here?"

"Gritu and Malzod have raised the shield again around the fortress. They have also reported false information about our escape. They're on our side."

"Wudak?"

Finn shakes his head.

"Wudak," I say quietly. I feel his loss in my soul.

Tilly and Scout stride into the room. I can see the rawness in their eyes. They have been crying. They both hold my right hand together.

Then come Theo and Nya, Biscuit, Zoe and Doc.

Everybody except Damian. I don't want to let the pain take over. Not right now.

"Freya, there's something that you need to know," Finn says.

"What?"

"Zolkon survived. He's our prisoner. He says he has some important information, but he will talk only to you."

"And then can we kill him?" I say, groggily.

I don't know why, but this makes every Savior laugh quietly.

I nod and close my eyes. Gritu brings Zolkon into the room. Everyone exits. Zolkon is in chains and in bad shape, but Doc said he'll live. I ask Finn to stay. I don't want to be alone with this monster.

Zolkon looks at me. "I hear you performed a miracle," he says, and his horrible laughter follows soon afterward.

"Buddy, laugh again, and I'm going to kill you."

I lift my hand and the receptor flies across the room and plants itself firmly in my grasp. Zolkon stops laughing. Finn rolls his eyes and takes the receptor out of my hand.

"I think it'd be better for you if we were alone when we talked," Zolkon says, looking at Finn.

"Not an option. Trust me. You don't want him to leave. He just saved your life."

"Very well. I want to make a deal with you. In exchange for my freedom, I will tell you all you need to know about your Sliman. And I don't mean Wudak."

"What does that mean?" I say, not liking the tone in his voice one bit.

"You didn't know? Your friend, the one who was captured, he's a Sliman."

"What on earth are you talking about?" Finn says.

"Well, he's a different model, an experimental one. To this day, nobody knew one of the experiments had survived and thrived without the Omicron 5. Now the aliens know. That's why they took him."

"You're insane," I say.

"Am I? Haven't you noticed anything different about him? His strength? His determination? His coldness and severity? His ease with violence? Let me guess, he told you that he loved you. Of course, he did. All Sliman are conditioned to love you."

I want to vomit or die. I think dying would be more graceful.

"We wouldn't be Sliman if we didn't love you. Not you specifically, but every Lagerian host. It's like we have a chip in our brains that turns on the moment your hands touch us deliberately. That's what happened to Wudak, that's why he died for you. And your lad, once he touched you the first time, he grew to love you. He didn't understand it. He might have fought it, but he could not resist."

My mind wanders now to the day of my escape. Damian's strong arms around me, carrying me through the woods, my hand on his neck. He would not let go.

"Even *I* felt a little jolt when you first walked in here. And you're not so bad on the eyes either. Am I right, boy?"

Finn glances to Zolkon vacantly. "Freya?"

Zolkon shakes his head at Finn. "Youth is wasted on the wrong people."

"Why not you, then?" Finn asks.

"I am too intelligent, too old to be caught in the web

the Lagerians have woven into my cells." He laughs again, and he's lucky my mind wanders back to Damian. Every moment we shared.

I glance at Finn. Will I ever tell him what Damian and I shared? What dark secret awaited him?

"Your friend and Wudak, they both bonded with you through touching you. Wudak knew what he was doing, the idiot. Your friend probably didn't. He didn't know that the price would be his own life."

My head hurts, and I reach out for Finn's hand. He takes it and rubs it with his, reassuring me he's here.

"He is the ultimate Sliman," Zolkon goes on, "the model they have been trying to create ever since they came to this planet. But unlike Sliman, he doesn't need Omicron 5 to stay alive. They hadn't predicted that. They might tear him apart limb by limb trying to discover how it happened."

"Shut up," I yell. "I don't care what's in his genes. He's human, you monster. Human! Born to a human mother. Willing to die for his fellow man."

"He will be what he was destined to be," Zolkon goes on as if he didn't hear a word I said. "A weapon. As will his child."

He pauses as if he's waiting for his words to sink in, but I have no reaction. I don't react to anything anymore, especially the words of a madman.

"I know you don't know it yet, but you will. Soon

enough. Wudak acted shocked when he saw the results on the analyzer. You were already carrying an embryo, one with human, Lagerian and Sliman markers. But we both know that he knew the truth. And now so does your young champion here."

My cheeks burn up. I look at Finn and I see death on his ghostly face. His noble features, his calmness, his composure are all but gone. He stares at me as a trapped animal would. I turn my eyes away. He knows I can't tell him that Zolkon is lying. He knows there's a possibility his words are true. He knows.

"It's a lie. Why would you ever offer the truth to me?"

"My dear girl, there are three things that I would never do. Tell the truth when nobody wants to reward me for it. Lie when I can't benefit from it. Pretend I care about the difference between the truth and a lie."

Finn staggers back and leans against a table.

"This is what I propose," Zolkon says. "If you let me go, I will contact my connections within the alien network and have them kill this Damian before he is tortured and brainwashed. What do you think? Isn't it a fair deal?"

"Shut your filthy mouth," Finn yells as he pounces on Zolkon and beats down on him with all his force.

"Finn," I say, but he doesn't listen. He punches Zolkon repeatedly until the old Sliman tumbles down to the ground, bloodied and half-conscious.

My best friend comes to me and takes me in his arms.

His warmth soothes my aches. He kisses my forehead quickly, but then he lets go too fast.

He grabs Zolkon by the hair and drags him out of my room.

◈

Gritu and Malzod have brought us back to the base. I can feel their guilt in the way their eyes won't quite meet mine. They didn't join the fight, but they couldn't. Keeping their involvement secret was the only way to protect the insurgency. They believe we'll be safe here for a while. Finn found Shy Boy hiding in the fortress garden, shaking with fear at the loud racket of the drones and the battle. We think he'll be okay. He carried me most of the way back.

I lie on my bed and stare at the ceiling. I have been in this position for two days. I have found that I can block out thoughts by concentrating on a small detail for hours. It numbs my brain to oblivion. I close my eyes, and I see his face again. Why did I forget that I'm not allowed to close my eyes anymore?

I make the decision in an instant. I get up, put my boots on, and walk down the hallway until I reach his door. I open it cautiously as if I could disturb him somehow with my indiscretion.

I bury my face in his pillow. I smell his scent and think

of all the times I told him to stay away from me and my tears flow freely finally. I can't keep the pain inside any longer. I know the truth now. I know that I don't want to live without him in my life. I can't live without our arguments. I can't live without hating his brute manners. I can't live without loving him.

But I have to live in darkness now. And I have to live knowing that I will never be able to tell him that I love him. My knees buckle under me. I fall to the floor, holding the pillow. I cry with loud sobs. I cry like it is the only thing left to do in the world.

"Freya?" Pip says.

I turn, startled, and see her standing in the doorway.

"It's okay," I say, wiping away tears and snot. "I'm fine."

"Freya. I know where they have taken him."

My senses get alerted all at the same time. "How could you, Pip?"

"It's all in my head again," she says. "I remember everything."

◆

About the Author

Stella Fitzsimons was born in Athens, Greece, and lives in Southern California with her husband and two sons. After studying economics and language arts she went on to teach both Mathematics and English before launching *Stella's Literary Bistro*, a bilingual literary journal. Her works include: *Forest Runners, The Dark Legion, The Shadow Empire, The Vanishing Tome, Luna, Winter, Silver Dust, Shadow Fall, Moonlight Mist* and *The Last Rider.*